HIRAM GRANGE

& the Digital Eucharist

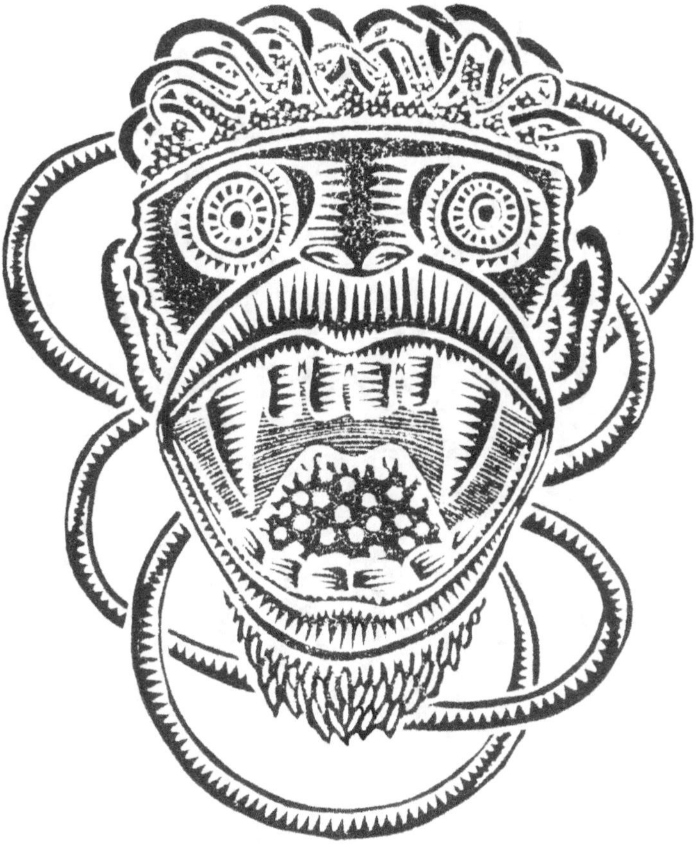

THE SCANDALOUS MISADVENTURES OF HIRAM GRANGE
BOOK 3

HIRAM GRANGE

& the Digital Eucharist

by

Robert Davies

SHROUD

SHROUD PUBLISHING
MILTON, NH

Robert Davies

HIRAM GRANGE
& the Digital Eucharist

from
Shroud Publishing

You are holding a limited edition small press novella in your hands.
This book is a result of hard work and creative effort.
Enjoy it, and celebrate the possibility of all things.

First Edition

First Printing April 2010
Copyright © 2010 Shroud Publishing
All Rights Reserved

Editor: Tim Deal
Cover & Interior Paintings by Malcolm McClinton
Book Design, Copy-editing & Illustrations by Danny Evarts
Additional Line-editing by Jim Elliott

The text of this book was composed using Adobe Garamond Pro.
Display type was set in Cracked and Charlemagne Std.

ISBN: 978-0-9819894-9-5

Shroud Publishing LLC
121 Mason Road
Milton, NH 03851
www.shroudmagazine.com

~DEDICATION~

For Sara, as always.

Prologue

The demon Giblis struggled against the warding circle that imprisoned it in a globe of shining light. A breathing marriage of scaled flesh and flame, Giblis shone with a bloody incandescence. Its skin was a thin veil over the malevolence seething just underneath. Tears in its flesh allowed the virulent flame to burn through. Born in the numberless days before starlight, it was a servant of the Abyss. It had been summoned into this world of stone and water, this legendary Earth, carried on a hot, frothy tide of blood and organic detritus, knowing only hunger and avarice and malice.

It was all for nothing. The Adepts who had summoned it were now dead.

"Odin's Third Nut! What are you two waiting for? Finish the casting and send it back to the Abyss!" said Hiram Grange.

"Laissez les bon temps rouler, eh, Grange?" Bale Laveaux was laughing. Careful not to disturb the chalk sigils of the warding circle, the mercenary kicked the bound demon. He leaned in to peer at its grotesque, reptilian face and spit a gobbet of phlegm in its right eye. The demon's neck muscles grew taut as it renewed its futile struggle. "C'mon, Elise, love, Grange want dat demon sent back."

Elise had the body of an angel, the darkest sense of humor Hiram had ever come across, and a malicious need to mercilessly tease him with her perfect cleavage. She was also a voudoun priestess, particularly skilled in the darker arts, both venereal and sanguinary.

Hiram swallowed, watching the young demon writhe in fury. The bastard was big. The globe of the binding spell cast off hot sparks that trailed blue fire. The air thrummed with energy. Ozone burned his nose. Hiram scanned the warding sigils again; he was certain that the bindings would hold. The last of the demons would be sent back to the hell that had given it birth.

It had all happened so fast. They had reached the abandoned subway station just as the Seven Adepts of Quo were completing the summoning ritual. Gertz's information had been right on the money. And the mercenary couple Gertz had recommended had performed admirably, even if Laveaux was a bit too intent on impressing Elise. The perils of young love.

The three of them had slipped into the abandoned subterranean station and followed the flickering of torches and the sounds of chanting until they reached the West platform. Without a word, they had unleashed a hail of gunfire, Hiram's trusted Webley Mk VI roaring three times, and dropped the adepts where they stood. There was no time for witty banter or idle threats when demons were involved. Two of the demons had been crushed as the confluence tunnels they were worming through slammed shut when the adept summoning them had his throat blown apart. Bloody slabs of meat and the sour reek of sulfur were all that remained.

The last demon was now imprisoned within the warding circle the Seven had set up, its summoning wards overlaid with Elise's voodoo binding sigils. The red-robed corpse of the High Adept lay at the demon's feet within the confines of the circle, his face destroyed by a bullet.

The air was thick with the scent of cordite and coppery blood. The corpses of the six other summoners lay on the ground, nothing more than bullet-riddled heaps. All that remained was to reopen the confluence, cast Giblis back to the Abyss, and then seal it with a kiss.

Across the circle from Hiram, Laveaux kicked the demon again, drawing blood.

Elise began the final incantation, a sooty gris-gris in her hand. The demon shivered in its confinement. Already the eternal chill of the Abyss was pouring through the opening confluence, frost crystals forming on the corpse at its feet. Steaming urine ran down the demon's scaly legs as it wailed; tears filled its eyes and sizzled on its cheeks.

Hiram let out a breath, relaxing for the first time in days. It had been his first mission since Sadie's death, and he hadn't been sure he could do it. He didn't know if he could do anything at all. Simply breathing was difficult without her in the world. He had spent months in the darkness of his Airstream trailer, drinking nothing more than orange juice, popping nothing more than vitamins, and yet every morning he awoke with intense splitting headaches and barely enough energy to reach the toilet. Days became weeks became months, and still she was gone.

Nevertheless, at Bothwell's insistence and with Clifford Gertz's help, Hiram had managed to pull this mission together. He'd needed some help, sure, but a win was a win. Sadie had taught him that little truth. It felt like an immense weight off his shoulders. Hiram actually wanted to laugh.

He holstered his Webley, the phantom heft of the suicide shell jolting him. His mother had killed herself with that shell. Hiram left the blank cartridge chambered as a reminder that a part of him had died that day, too. Damn, Hiram thought, he was getting maudlin again. He needed some Thai food and some vintage porn, stat. He had not given up all his vices.

The bound demon was still pissing itself in fear. The poor bastard was like a goddamn racehorse, filling the smoky chamber with the biting stench of its urine. It was afraid. Hiram was glad to know that a demon from the Abyss was still afraid of him. He still had what it took. He was back. He thought Sadie would approve.

Elise fell silent; her eyes widened. Time seemed to telescope then, everything drawing close and clear, moving in slow motion. Sounds rang distant, echoing.

"It's wiping away the sigils!"

The bubbling pool of demon piss was yellow, tinged with cloudy threads of blood, on the dusty cement floor. It quickly spread toward the colored chalk symbols, engulfing the eldritch letters, dissolving them and swallowing their light. The circle was breached. The powerful thrumming of the binding globe was snuffed out. For a moment, everything was still.

The silence that filled the chamber was the quietus before cataclysm, the indrawn breath before a final scream. The air was tense with the waiting of it all. Hiram could not breathe. Cotton packed his ears and thin needles of anticipation prodded at his eyelids.

Giblis began to laugh. It was a guttural, harsh sound.

Everything went to hell.

Chapter One

Hiram Grange sucked in pipe smoke as he watched pigeons pecking at frozen vomit on the asphalt, his thoughts again going back to that hellish night beneath the city years ago. The February night air chilled him. His father's old black suit was ill-fitting and did little to shield his thin body from the cold. The asphalt was white with salt, but the mounded snow banks were gray and hard, cold tumors impregnated with shopping carts, newspapers, and the bent spines of umbrellas waiting patiently for late May to give them up in the thaw.

It was stark madness that sent him from the pleasing warmth of the bar and his half-filled bottle of Harpoon IPA, from the bevy of pliable tattooed co-eds that flittered around his table like drunken moths, but apparently smoking was not allowed inside the hallowed walls of the *Leftist Lounge*. Madness! Still, despite the razoring New England cold, the blessed blend of Presbyterian Mixture and Thailand Ghost filled Hiram with the burning clean oblivion he needed now. He bit down on his briarwood pipe and sucked in another lungful of warm, bitter smoke, feeling it soften the edges of reality.

He didn't like this city. There were too many memories, too many nightmares, and not enough drugs and whiskey to keep them at bay. Bothwell had coaxed him back by saying it was a routine job—well, as routine as could be expected considering he dealt with some seriously fucked up shit. He just wanted to get it over with and move on.

Out of the corner of his eye, Grange watched a homeless

man approaching, shivering beneath the grimy layers of a Red Sox jersey and a Members Only jacket with a broken zipper. He walked with one foot on the sidewalk, one on the street, his head weighted down with such a mass of filthy, dreadlocked hair that it seemed to threaten to snap his spine. The man paused before the abandoned church across the street, just beneath a vast verdigrised Jesus statue crowned in thorns of bird shit.

He turned and moved toward Hiram, reaching out a hand.

"He is coming for you," the man said. His voice raw, his yellow eyes gleaming with fever. "He is coming for us all."

Hiram, pleasantly buzzing now, looked up at the frozen crucified messiah.

"By Kali's Second Slit, he'd better hurry it up." Hiram reached into his pocket, removed a few folded bills, and handed them to the prophet. "By my tally, the bastard owes me quite a few drinks." He tapped out the spent ashes, pocketed his pipe, ran a hand through his long, greasy hair, and returned to the frantic warmth of the bar.

His table, nestled in the corner near one of the loudspeakers, was no longer empty. Mrs. Bothwell was sitting across from Hiram's seat, her hands folded in front of her. She was overdressed for the Lounge, and Hiram caught the scent of Chanel #5 before he even sat down. Her eyes were as bright as ever.

"You could look pleased to see me sometime," Bothwell said, smiling.

"Charmed. It's getting late."

"I see you are still in a mood. Very well. What do you know of the Occlusionist Movement?"

The Movement was relatively new as it came to cults. It had sprouted up about five years earlier, a savvy mix of New

Age healing, self-actualization, sci-fi gibberish, and Hollywood celebrity. The only reason they were on Hiram's radar at all is that they had tried to recruit Jodie Foster a few years ago.

It had been a very small fringe group until about a year ago, when a new leader emerged with claims that he had been given the Vision of the Ancients. Soon after, several high-profile executives, politicians, and military officers publicly announced their allegiance to the Movement. CEOs from the android conglomerate TikTok Industries, Mindware Corporation, and the military corporation Defensor had joined in recent months, along with several of the hottest Hollywood celebrities.

The Movement quickly made a name for itself around the globe. It had just recently finished construction of the Occlusionist Tower, its international headquarters in downtown Boston, a glass monstrosity that jutted into the sky like a well-polished urban dildo.

"I'm not sure why you care about it," Hiram said. "It seems a little outside my realm of expertise."

"Microconfluences," Bothwell said. The word hung in the air between them. Hiram felt something at the base of his spine uncoil, a gelid serpent of fear. "They are tiny. Brief. The sensors barely detect them at all. There were scattered reports of them occurring across the country for several months, but the lab jockeys were never able to pin anything down until now.

"Lately, it seems that Boston is ground zero for them. Mainly, the Occlusionist Tower. They are increasing, in both number and duration. I need you to investigate. What is causing them? Why?"

Hiram cursed and threw back the remainder of his beer. He really needed to get back to the Airstream, where he always kept a bottle of the good stuff. Bothwell grinned, knowingly. Hiram knew that look. Bothwell wasn't done.

"There is a rumor that the Occlusionists are involved with Mindware. They have had some kind of breakthrough with the technology. We have reason to think the two may be related. And considering where the Occlusionists built their tower, it could very well be a big deal." Bothwell slid a thick packet across the table. "All that we know is in there. The next steps are up to you."

"Excellent."

"There's one last thing."

"Always is with you."

"It seems your friend Laveaux has some information he is eager to share. Something to do with that night."

"You're joking."

"He said he will only share it with you."

"He wants to kill me, Bothwell. You know that."

"Don't let him." Bothwell smiled. "Here's the address he gave me. I suspect the place is less luxurious than this one."

Bothwell left without another word.

Hiram tossed back his nightcap, letting the pitifully bad music—some bubble gum shit filtered through Autotune—take him where it would, letting his ears ring and his stomach burn. All around him kids talked and laughed, their mouths opening, their voices lost in the raucous din that was the animal of crowds, that gestalt beast that man seemed to aspire to, their painted mouths small little Os of pleasure and laughter and seduction and lies and desperation. Openings between the wide night of endless possibilities and the cold, dark morning of sticky, sore regret.

Microconfluences.

Christ! He needed to put on a Jodie Foster flick and interrogate the suspect, tout de suite. After some pills. And a smoldering pipe. And a few more nightcaps. He needed to hide, to crawl into the emptiness of oblivion before he was steeled enough to dive into the serious shit storm that was brewing here.

"How are things proceeding, sir? Second time will be the charm?"

"Remarkably well, General. Grange has been drawn back again. Perhaps this time we can really get things to work. He is never able to resist it seems."

"He suspects nothing?"

"He suspects the wrong thing. He looks at the sun while we dig in the dirt."

"I am … uneasy. The demon will be difficult to control."

"I have no intention of controlling it. I want it free."

"That was not the plan we discussed."

"My plans have changed."

"Grange could still be a threat to us if he learns too much."

"Then all these years of, ah, nurturing will have finally paid off."

Chapter Two

On the abandoned platform of the Downtown Mission subway station, five cooling corpses formed a meticulous circle of outstretched limbs and broken necks. Each chest had been splayed open, the pale skin peeled back and the rib cages cracked and split. Several glistening organs had been plucked out and placed at various points along the circumference of the warding circle. Wet lengths of blue-black intestine snaked around each nude corpse, twining with those of the next body, binding them all together. At each of the four compass points, 7-11 Big Gulp cups held a frothy syrup of blood and semen. Nineteen flickering Yankee Candles filled the abandoned station with the reek of lilacs, frankincense, and burnt citrus.

At the center of this summoning circle, naked and sweating, buzzing with Red Bull, cocaine, and amphetamines, nervously muttering the incantations he had struggled for weeks to memorize, stood Roger Millis—48 years old, balding, hen-pecked husband, father of five, and self-proclaimed adept of the Art.

Millis had learned that the veil between realities was perilously thin here, worn away by atrocities, murder and mayhem. It had been so bad that the authorities abandoned the entire station and sealed off the tunnels. A few years ago, there had been a failed attempt to summon three demons from the Abyss. Millis knew he would succeed where the others had failed, for this was his destiny. He was the chosen one, the Reverse Messiah, and soon he would get what was coming to him.

Millis was beginning the last quatrain of the Grand Summoning when he saw a man walking up the train tracks from the darkness beyond, whistling and twirling an ebony cane. The stranger's immaculate white linen suit and hat practically shone. Millis watched, stunned, as the man effortlessly leapt from the tracks onto the platform and sauntered toward the warding circle, clicking his cane on the concrete with every step.

The man in white took in the scene, walking around the circle, sardonically shaking his head. "This is sloppy work, Mr. Millis. Sloppy work indeed."

Millis felt his insides go cold. He found he could not move.

"Ah, I've been terribly rude. The name is Cascade. My timetable had to be moved up a little, so I am here to speed things along. We have need of your little friend sooner than I anticipated. Still, this is barely passable slaughter, Mr. Millis."

Cascade pointed with his cane.

"Look, here you have the position of the organs all wrong. Cooling lungs have a stronger influence on the pneuma when placed on the left. And here, look! Kidneys should never, ever face the south. Children know that." He paused at one of the corpses. "This looks like the work of an epileptic butcher. Christ! These incisions are brutal. Where's your sense of art? Where's your pride, man?"

Cascade knelt down, grabbed a corpse's head, and turned it to see her face. "Ah, she does look like Ms. Foster, doesn't she? At least you did that right. They all could pass for his beloved Jodie in the right lighting. I pray Grange sees them before their flesh wilts. Oh, what it would have been to have the real Jodie Foster for the Summoning. I think Grange would positively shatter. Alas, these dispatched strumpets will have to do."

He then knelt at the edge of the summoning circle. "But this is simply unforgivable. These summoning words you have used. The letters are barely decipherable."

Millis found the last remnant of his spine. "What do you know of the Golden Helico Text?" He had emptied out his 401K and his daughters' college funds, and had to sell all his coins and Civil War memorabilia to scrape together enough money for it.

"Well, for starters, I own the original copy," Cascade said.

Millis was shocked to silence.

"It proved invaluable when I made the forgery that you came across. That I, ah, allowed you to find."

Millis felt his mouth go dry.

"Oh, yes, it was a masterwork, if I can be so crass as to congratulate myself. I chewed the insects myself to get the ink color correct, and I flayed three lambs for their perfect skin. An exact copy, down to the carved bone frontispiece. Of course, I tweaked the text a little, shuffled a few names around, and tainted a few spells."

Millis felt ice filling his veins. "What have you done to me?"

"To you? Not a thing. You are merely cheese in the trap, old boy. An ambitious little snack that is going to summon a really big mouse. What *it* does to you? Well, I trust that will not be pleasant at all."

Millis could not control his shaking now. He could barely breathe. Speaking was a labor. "I just wanted a succubus."

Cascade laughed again. "So you have scrawled here; in your blood and seed, no less. This truly is pathetic. One does not summon demons using the empty letters of the alphabet. Those letters pass the mouths of morons, lovers, and priests every single day. No, you need something more. Look! That is what you needed, there, and those sigils there."

Strange, bright runes rose slightly from the spaces between the letters Millis had written. They writhed with dark, organic power. "Those are the bleeding letters of the Omegabet, the tongue of the final star. I took the liberty of seeding your little cantrip with them. Put a different worm on the hook, as it were. Face it, old boy, you're summoning a fish for the ages. Something old."

Millis' eyes ached as the glowing letters pulsed, throbbing at a cardiac pace. To his horror, the hearts of the five corpses began to pulse in time with the letters' brightness. Atrophied, rigored muscles began to snap and move, and bloody hands slid across the concrete until they found vaginas as cold as oysters. With frantic intensity, the dead worried at themselves, sucking in air through slit throats. Globules of clotted blood began to float and move in spirals around the shining circle.

Millis read the name of the demon, burning among the letters. "Giblis," he whispered. Hot piss ran down his legs.

"Got it on the first try! The very one," Cascade said. "He's one of the Unmakers, I do believe. A bit out of your league, little adept. Nevertheless, he is on his way, and I trust he will be a tad ravenous."

"What is it you want from me? Please."

"Oh, don't be silly. This is not a bartering session. You are a dead man. That is quite out of my hands."

He removed a small pouch from an inside pocket. Out of it he pulled a bullet and laid it on the edge of the circle. He took a few steps and dropped three caps from absinthe bottles. The last thing he pulled from the pouch was a tattered scrap of cloth.

He sniffed it and grimaced. "Your taste in cologne was always so gauche, Hiram Grange." He dropped the cloth inside the circle.

Reaching into another pocket, he removed a small origami scorpion. Spinning it in his fingers before dropping it inside the circle, he turned to leave.

"Wait! Where are you going? What is this?"

Cascade grinned. "Nothing you need concern yourself with. Just a friendly message to the demon for when it is born."

"B-b-born?"

"You did not read the Helico Text to the end, did you?" The man in white laughed one last time. "Just remember. Deep breaths, old boy. Deep breaths."

Bale Laveaux was silent as he ate his dinner, pausing every now and then to wipe remoulade sauce from his lip with a napkin and sip from a glass of ice water. When Hiram had entered Grendel's Den, Laveaux had called him over to a corner table. He told Hiram to order quickly because the half-priced menu shut off after 7 p.m.

Hiram was more than curious, but he was feeling indulgent and was content to let Laveaux set the pace. He sipped at his Dogfish 60 Minute IPA and took another bite of the fiery shrimp sambal. It was surprisingly good and spicy considering he was in the heart of Harvard Square. It was a blazing masterpiece, even if the chef may have gone a tad overboard with the turmeric.

Laveaux nodded when the waitress offered to take his empty plate away.

"You ready to talk?"

Laveaux grinned.

Hiram stood. "I am tired of games."

Laveaux held up a hand. "I forgot. Patience is not a strong suit with you."

His face darkened and he clenched a fist on top of the table.

"We all lost something that day, mon ami," Laveaux said. "It can't happen again." Laveaux gestured, taking in the small bar, the entire city, but Hiram knew he was really talking about the abandoned subway station where they had dispatched three demons from the Abyss.

Hiram sat down.

Laveaux slid a picture across the table. "Jeremiah Stromm, the *First Among the Vision*, the leader of the Occlusionist Movement."

"Yeah, I've heard of him. Recluse. Eccentric."

"You've met him before." Laveaux smiled. It was not a pleasant smile. "Beneath the city."

"What the hell are you talking about?"

"Stromm was one of the Seven."

Hiram stared at the picture, but there was nothing in the old, wizened face that he recognized.

"The Seven all died. I killed three of them myself."

"Yes, you did. I killed two. Elise got two. Stromm was the last to fall, if I recall correctly. He was the High Adept."

"You can't be serious. There wasn't even a body left."

Laveaux shook his head. "If I didn't hate you so much, I would feel bad for you."

Hiram cursed, his thoughts going back to the chaos of that night. How could a dead man return from the Abyss?

"I also came across this." Laveaux slid a small wooden box across the table. "I was tempted to throw it away, but I know you are a dabbler."

Hiram flipped open the lid of the small box. It was filled with dried green and red leaves, nestled in a shallow bed of pink powder.

"Said it was called Scorpion Kiss or some such."

Hiram was at a loss for words. This was not what he had expected.

"Well, I'm just a messenger these days. I am done."

Laveaux stood and leaned heavily against the table. He pulled a crutch off the bench and shifted his weight onto it. His left leg was a mere stub, wrapped in a tied-off pant leg. He had lost it that night in the steaming belly of the city.

The sight of the missing leg almost brought the horror back, but Hiram was not ready for that. Not now. Hiram wasn't sure he would ever be ready to face what he'd done that night.

He turned away, felt his mouth go dry.

"Christ," Hiram said. "Let me buy you a drink."

"I don't touch the stuff anymore," Laveaux said, shaking his head. "Booze makes me crave the taste of my gun far too much."

Laveaux took a few halting steps and then turned.

"Hiram, she might have forgiven you for what you did," he said. "But I never will."

It would have been better if Laveaux had punched him in the gut or slammed the wooden crutch into his face. It couldn't have felt any worse. It would have been preferable to the darkness that was spreading inside, the chill of regret he could not ignore.

Hiram watched Laveaux slowly make his way out of the bar, drawing stares from everyone he passed. Still shaken, Hiram caught the eye of a cute waitress. She had a pierced face, ample breasts, and a Chinese symbol tramp stamp. He gave her the peace sign, mouthing "Two more."

Laveaux had lost a leg because of Hiram. Elise had died.

Sadie died, too. All because of him. He was far too dangerous.

Every day, when he looked in the mirror, Hiram remembered the loss of Sadie; felt it shift, stretch, and curl up inside him, breathing.

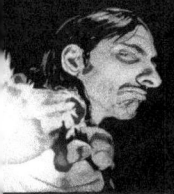

Chapter Three

B ack in the blessed, safe confines of his Airstream trailer, parked in a convenient spot down by the waterfront, Hiram spilled the contents of the packet Bothwell had given him onto the table.

There were several manila folders filled with photocopied pages and chicken-scratch notations; a thin, but detailed report on the most recent microconfluence detections; a sparse dossier on Jeremiah Stromm, the enigmatic leader of the Occlusionist Movement and, if Laveaux was to be believed, a corpse who returned from the Abyss with a bit more pep in his step; a laminated key card marked with a glowing brain, the logo of the Mindware Corporation; and a DVD in a plastic case.

Hiram spent several hours reviewing the material, slotting it in with what he had learned from Laveaux. It still made little sense.

He picked up the DVD case. It was unlabeled. Could Bothwell have been so kind as to have found of copy of the rumored Jodie Foster sex tape?

Hiram prayed for small mercies as he slipped the disc into his laptop. He was quickly disappointed. The video was clear, but the audio was soft and had a distinct echo, probably due to the location of the camera, lodged in what had to be an air vent. The view was from up high, looking down and to the left over a long, polished oak conference table with at least nine plush leather seats visible. Some of the table was cut off from the field of view, but judging by its arc, there were probably three to five more people seated out of sight. The video was date-stamped from over a month ago.

Standing at regular intervals around the table were white-faced android geishas in stylized short red robes, still as statues, waiting to be needed.

Jeremiah Stromm stood at the head of the table, his right hand raising a glass of what looked like wine, a shimmering ruby that caught the light from the chandeliers. The picture Laveaux had shown him must be recent. Stromm was old, but elegant, with features of the perfect politician and the perfect televangelist. His white hair was meticulously shorn. Even his suit was cut in such a fashion as to evoke the sense of a ritualistic robe, the tails on his coat longer than normal, the cuffs deeper and more pronounced. Even in the less than optimal footage from the video feed, he looked perfect. Hiram could only imagine that he smelled like Ivory soap and summer mornings.

"I'd like to make a toast!"

Everyone on the video grew silent. Gathered around the table were what seemed to be an elite crowd. Hiram even recognized a few, some from television, some from the Internet; a few had dossiers in the packet. Two female newscasters from the local news channels; Felicity Caldwell, the upstart socialite famous for seducing two of her teachers, and her principal, at the tender age of thirteen and posting the lurid clips online; Camper Brace, the star catcher for the Red Sox; Jeffrey Cox, visiting conductor of the Boston Symphony Orchestra; Brian Cooper, the CEO of TikTok Industries.

"I look out at you, fellow Visionaries, and see the future. Not a future of wealth, or conquest, or infamy, for those things we all have in abundance, no?" His smile was radiant. "It is a new future, one that only the few can envision, that only the few can ever hope to see."

He walked around the table as he spoke, conscious of all eyes on him. "All too often we allow the negative thoughts of others to cloud the truth, to hide our potential, to occlude the possible." He walked off the edge of the screen, rounding the hidden side of the table, but his voice could still be heard. "You all have learned to break through that, to become more."

"Once opened, the Eye of Vision is never closed," said one of the newscasters. A few others murmured the same platitude.

Stromm was nodding as he entered the frame on the other side of the table. "You all were brave enough to be able to open that hidden eye. Tonight you will see the Vision that started me on this glorious path. And to celebrate I have had this fine vintage taken from the cellars."

"Gentlemen, ladies," Stromm began. "Please raise your glasses. Moments such as this are rare and should be savored."

He eyed each follower in turn, smiling, nodding. He tilted his head and grinned, raising his glass high.

"Drink to the Vision!"

After sipping deeply, Felicity Caldwell recapitulated perhaps her most famous scene as what was likely cyanide made her mouth violently foam white froth as she spasmed. Beside her, the two newscasters slumped down in their chairs. The others were shocked to silence, staring at their own drinks.

A man put his glass down and pushed his chair back. Two android geishas stood behind him, preventing him from standing.

"You haven't had any wine, Mr. Underwood," Jeremiah Stromm said. "Come, come. Everyone else has had his or her wine. Only three were judged unworthy of the Vision. Surely, you are one of us now. Are you not?"

Underwood's eyes darted from his glass to the others in the room.

Hiram was astounded to see how quickly the shock of three deaths had gone from their faces. They had passed! They were going to be initiated into the Omega Level of the Occlusionist Movement. Surely, not everyone was destined for such greatness, surely those three were unfit. Hiram knew the type all too well. They began to stare at Underwood with a feral malice, as though each second he hesitated was an affront to their bright new day.

Their eyes seemed to be saying, "*Join us!*" and "*Die!*" It seemed they wanted both in equal measure.

"Mr. Underwood," Stromm said. "Surely, your wine has breathed enough."

Underwood reached for his glass and gulped its contents down. "*Hold!*"

Hiram jerked in his seat; the volume of the command seemed much louder than the earlier spoken words, more clear. Stromm was now staring directly into the remote camera, a thin smile on his face. "It appears we have unwelcome guests who wish to impinge on our affairs. No matter. Behold the Vision!"

Jeremiah Stromm then reached up and placed a hand across his face, gripping and twisting. He removed the skin to reveal a brilliant whiteness to the camera before the screen faded to gray, idiot snow. The only thing that remained was the time stamp in bold white letters: 7:35 p.m., October 20.

Hiram poured himself a whiskey and flipped through the papers that were scattered on his table. So, not everyone was welcome into the highest echelons of the Movement. And it wasn't a simple 'no thanks, here's the door,' either. The only way out of the Movement once you knew its secrets was apparently death.

Then Hiram saw it, among the record of microconfluences: nine detections lasting an average of thirty-five seconds, commencing October 20, 7:31 p.m. The final microconfluence had opened at 7:36 p.m. and closed twenty seconds later. The three dead women were not involved, then; it was those that the Movement accepted. The microconfluences were caused by them.

That must have been one hell of a vintage, Hiram thought. What were they really doing in that Tower?

He checked his watch. It was time to do some reconnaissance.

Chapter Four

T he Occlusionist Tower rose toward the sky, jutting from the surrounding buildings, a glass monolith. The entrance way was opulent, with wide stairs rising to sliding glass doors.

Hiram watched the front door from his vantage point on the third level of a parking garage across the street. The concrete structure did little to shield him from the fierce cold. Even wedged as he was between two SUVs, the night air assailed him. He hated being outside like this. He longed for the comfort and solitude of his trailer. At this hour the sidewalks were much emptier, peopled only by wayward youths and homeless veterans; during the day the stores and streets would be bustling. Now it was too quiet. It was too open. Too free. He felt exposed, naked even.

Hiram wore a leather pouch around his neck. It contained a small carved lodestone that could detect the electromagnetic energies given off by a nearby confluence. Bothwell could have provided him with a more elaborate technical device, but it would not have been shielded and might be picked up by the building's security systems. Hiram had his suspicions already about what he was looking for, and a coldness turned in his stomach. This little stone would help get confirmation.

Limousines and black town cars drove up to the main entrance, disgorging men in tuxedos and gorgeous women in tight-fitting designer dresses and glinting jewels, before slipping off up Washington Street to the Boston Common. Conspicuously absent were the flash of cameras from paparazzi or the wailing screams of an adoring crowd. These elite folks moved with a quiet patience into the building, and alone or as couples ascended in the glass elevator, showing the city around them that they were the only ones rising to the top.

The parade of cars stopped at 7:35 p.m., when an elderly gentleman in impeccable clothing emerged from a limousine. It was Stromm. He moved quite well for a dead man.

Stromm waved off the offered help from the valets and servitors and slipped into the building. Hiram watched the elevator rise to the top floor and remain there. The lights inside darkened. The festivities were about to begin.

Hiram shivered as he waited.

It wasn't until 9:05 p.m. that the stone around his neck began to throb. This was something different, though, something Hiram had never encountered before. The confluences the stone detected were very small, and seemed to last for a minute at the longest, but they were extremely powerful. They flickered into existence with violence, like small exploding stars, and then vanished without a trace.

Hiram needed to get inside. He needed to see what was happening on the top floor. The Occlusionists were dealing with something they likely did not understand.

Or worse, Stromm knew all too well what he was doing.

Either way, Hiram had to stop them.

He had to stop them before it was too late.

Bale Laveaux limped into his stale, darkened bedsit.

Someone had been here. The hairs he always left on the doorjamb were gone.

But he didn't care. What could they do to him now? Still, he was tense for the moment it took him to realize that they'd already gone. The bathroom was barely illuminated with a cloying lemon-scented night light, and the neon sign from the bowling alley-slash-biker bar across the street cast its red and green glow across the stacked, stained mattresses on the linoleum. He was alone.

He flipped on the single, bright overhead bulb. The wattage was too much for the socket, but he had always liked to live dangerously. The room smelled like stale cigarettes, cayenne, and Tabasco sauce. A small dresser, covered with gris-gris, a top hat, bricks, a crushed cigar, candles, and a small stylized painting of Baron Saturday, was pressed up against the wall.

There were two packages, wrapped in plain brown paper, lying on the disheveled sheets. There was a card, too.

He knew there would be no fingerprints on any surface.

His heart started to beat a little faster. He was not sure if what he'd done was worth it. Still, Hiram had to pay. To suffer as much as he had.

Laveaux let himself fall to sit on the edge of the mattresses. His crutch fell and crashed to the floor. His phantom limb began to throb, his missing toes itched, his forgotten knee ached as though a thunderstorm were coming.

He pulled the larger of the two packages onto his lap and tested its weight before carefully unwrapping the brown paper, half expecting to see exposed wires. The silk-lined box held a bottle of aged bourbon.

He set it on the floor and then reached for the card.

It was blank on the front, the paper inside a creamy parchment. The script was meticulous, etched with burgundy ink.

"Your reward, as promised."

Folded inside the card was an origami alligator.

He let the card fall to the floor. His heart was pounding now. This was not what he had expected.

A man dressed in immaculate white clothes had knocked on his door weeks ago. He had come with a proposition.

"Hiram Grange has been a thorn in my side for some while now. It is time that he is chastised. I need your help."

"Why me?"

"You are a reminder that he is fallible. The guilt of that night gnaws at him. I want to pour some salt on that wound."

"Who are you? How do you know about that?"

The man in white shook his head.

"I also want you to give him this." He handed Laveaux a small wooden box.

Laveaux flipped the lid open and regarded the contents. "Opium?"

"Among other things," said the man in white. "It is the Scorpion's Kiss. It will bring Hiram to the edge. And whether he breaks or not, you can rest assured that it will not be pleasant at all for him. I will see to it that you are rewarded for your efforts."

Laveaux had agreed, and now it seemed that Grange was going to get what was coming to him. Oddly enough, he didn't feel all that much better. If possible, he felt worse.

He reached for the second, smaller box. Its weight surprised him. Something shifted as he hefted it. For a moment, he imagined a wild rodent inside, something alive seeking to be released.

He tore at the brown paper this time, careless, reckless. His ears were ringing. His mouth was dry. He felt as though he were being watched through the windows, through the walls, that the white ceiling itself was a vast, inquisitive eye. Everything seemed to be focused on him, on this moment.

He ripped through the tape that held the box closed and flipped open the two flaps. There was a gun inside.

A Jericho 941.

Laveaux caught his breath.

Elise.

It was her gun.

It was still covered in her dried blood.

Bale Laveaux lay the loaded gun beside him on the mattress, called for Papa Ghede, and reached for the bourbon.

Chapter Five

Hiram was exhausted. The morning sun hurt his eyes, and his throat was still raw from the bowls of opium he had squandered to give himself some semblance of sleep. But his mind had raced all night long, visions of pale, blind things worming their way through microconfluences filled his mind's eye every time he nodded off.

Hiram questioned whether entering the Occlusionist Tower was the wisest move, considering he'd once shot the Movement's leader in the face, killing him. But that night had been chaotic and dark, and he would be surprised if anyone had seen their faces through the blinding muzzle flashes and gun smoke. And it was very likely that it wasn't Stromm at all, merely someone, or something, that had borrowed his face. Hiram knew he could stand on the sidewalk all day weighing the pros and cons, but he needed to get inside and find out what was going on.

A crowd of animal rights protesters gathered outside the Occlusionist Tower, handing out leaflets, shouting slogans that steamed in the frigid air, and carrying signs. "*The Movement Kills*" read one. "*Really Open Your Eyes, Idiots!*" said another. Two beautiful girls held a banner between them that read, "*Mindware is Murder.*" One held a placard with an adorable chimpanzee staring ahead with a serving of steak tartare piled in its opened skull. Another wore a Curious George costume with an electrical socket and cord attached to the forehead.

"Do you know that the Occlusionist Movement tests its technologies on animals, sir?" A bright-eyed girl stood in front of

Hiram. "They murder innocent creatures in the pursuit of profit."

"I will definitely take a brochure on that," Hiram said. It had all been covered in the packet from Bothwell. The Mindware Corporation had been acquired recently by the Occlusionist Movement in a hostile takeover.

"You aren't going in there, are you?"

"I just have a few questions that need answering. I am as outraged with them as you are." Hiram, of course, had different reasons. Microconfluences! They were messing around with forces that should be left alone.

He crossed the street against the traffic and entered the lobby, where at least it was blessedly warm.

"Welcome to the Visitor Center! I am Kenneth."

Hiram reluctantly shook hands with the overly cheerful young man in the shiny Art Deco lobby of the Occlusionist Tower. His hands were moist. The man wore tan khakis and a blue polo shirt emblazoned with an open eye above his left breast. "What questions brought you to us today?"

"Curiosity, mostly." Hiram forced a smile. "I've heard so much on the news, but who can say? The people outside don't seem so thrilled with you."

Kenneth smiled again. "Ah, yes, I must say that the people and the media can often be close-minded in their dealings with the Movement. One of the main reasons we focus so much on community outreach with our Information Centers."

Hiram scanned the lobby as he spoke. There were large television screens on three of the walls, each filled with a close-up of Jeremiah Stromm speaking. It appeared to be a loop of his most common aphorisms, asking people to open then inner eye and see the truth, to embrace the reality of the world that was all around them. For a moment, Hiram felt as though Stromm were speaking directly to him. It was unnerving.

"What was the big commotion last night? I was passing by and thought there was a movie premiere or something."

Kenneth laughed. "It was a special day for the Movement. We inducted new members into the Omega Level. Paulina Verhoef and David Castle were among the few selected for elevation."

Hiram nodded. An induction ceremony, right around the time that his stone had started sensing microconfluences opening. They had to be related. Hiram was all too conscious that nearby, a few hundred yards below the ground, the Seven had attempted to summon three demons. In that place, the veil between this world and the Abyss had been worn precariously thin. Playing with confluences so close to it was insane. It was like lighting matches while standing in a puddle of gas.

"No way I could witness a ceremony, I suppose?"

More laughter from Kenneth. "I've been with the Movement for years and I have yet to see an Omega Induction. It takes long years of study and discipline before one can be judged worthy of ascension."

Action movie star David Castle was a tabloid fixture for his predilection for aged whiskey and underage girls, and was a notorious dabbler in quasi-faiths, being involved with Kabbalah, Scientology, ClearMindNow, and several other similar cults and organizations in the span of two years. He had joined the Movement only months before. Hiram pointed this out to the smiling Kenneth.

"There are those for whom the Movement is perfect, and it takes only their time of awakening to show them the way."

And their wallets, Hiram thought, but he said nothing. He

scanned the lobby again. The security was well concealed, but it quickly became clear that the Tower was less an office building than a fortress. Reinforced glass laced with Faraday strips to prevent electronic snooping. Mirrored walls and windows that must conceal security details and office spaces. Biometric sensors for the elevators and doors. Passive retinal scans and facial detection. That was all he could see, but he was sure there was much more still hidden. The security, like the elaborate landscaping and excessive open spaces, was a flaunting of wealth and importance.

"Are there any tours of the building?"

"Not as such," said Kenneth, still smiling. Hiram hoped it hurt to smile that much. "That is a perk reserved for Members."

"Well, I must say I am intrigued," Hiram said. "Perhaps I will take some literature and consider my options." He counted four cameras in small, innocuous dark globes. He considered dropping his trousers and mooning them, but they were probably decoys anyway. The real surveillance was probably done via x-ray, infrared, and such, all the more effective for being concealed.

Across the lobby, a young couple was talking softly and perusing the Movement literature. There was a large collection of colorful brochures detailing the history of the Movement, membership options, and the free pamphlet, "*The Top Ten Things You Can Do Right Now to See the Future.*" The couple looked over at him, smiling. Hiram noticed the faint but definite outline of guns beneath their jackets. There were many levels of security at the Tower, it seemed. Some all too visible.

On the walls, the screens continued their video loop, but Stromm's eyes were now definitely fixed on him, peering. Hiram felt like a specimen in a lab. The smiling, talking image of Stromm was somehow inspecting him.

"Thank you for taking time out of your day," Kenneth said. He had saved his very bestest smile for last. "Please don't hesitate to come back if you have any further questions. And remember, the Initiate's Tent is open on the Boston Common on Mondays and Thursdays. We'd love to see you there."

Hiram turned to leave.

"Ah, one moment," Kenneth raised a hand. He paused, his smile frozen. His eyes seemed to roll back in his head for a second. They focused again, peering at Hiram. The eyes were filled with a shining darkness now. "Mr. Hiram Grange. My master welcomes you to the Tower."

"Shit!"

Before he could react, Hiram was grabbed from behind. "Welcome!" The word was echoed by others as every head in the lobby turned toward him. All the eyes were filled with the same cold blackness. "Welcome, Hiram Grange." It became a chant, and they all moved toward him. The large images of Stromm on the screens laughed. They pushed in on Hiram, grabbing him, mindless in their singular intent. "I have plans for this world, Grange," said Stromm through the speakers. "Your bullets and your violence have no effect on the Vision. You will soon See!"

Glass shattered, followed quickly by raucous voices. A sudden cold wind filled the lobby. Hiram struggled against the arms holding him fast. An alarm sounded, a piercing klaxon accompanied by flashing red lights. Defensive gates slammed down in front of the three elevator bays, protecting the upper levels from the disturbance.

"Free the monkeys! Free the mind!"

The protesters had finally had enough of the cold and decided to bring their little demonstration indoors. Hiram thanked his good fortune, slamming an elbow into Kenneth's face and breaking those perfect teeth. A second blind punch landed with a satisfying crunch.

The lobby filled with chaos. One of the glass doors had been shattered. The black-eyed drones of the Movement attacking Hiram were quickly outnumbered by protesters carrying placards, overturning furniture and bookshelves, and spray-painting slogans across the walls. Someone threw a potted plant against one of the screens, shattering it.

A woman pulled Hiram from the madness of the crowd. "You should not be here. Run. Now, before they can summon more security." There was something familiar about her, a smell of lilacs, but there was too much confusion. Hiram tried to see her face, but she had blended into the maelstrom of the crowd. Hiram took his chance and ran.

"Grange was at the center of a disturbance at the Occlusionist Tower."

"Yes, I have heard," said Cascade. "It was much sooner than I had anticipated. He managed to escape, I take it?"

"Not without some help."

A video screen filled with images of the violent protest and the seemingly random decision to break into the lobby.

"That one there seems to be the ringleader. The red jacket."

"Blow up the face," Cascade said. "Yes, that's fine. It is her."

"You know her? Is she one of yours?"

"No, she is not one of mine. Not yet."

His mother had died in childbirth, and it was now clear that Roger Millis was going to do the same.

The constant pain had unhinged him from the atrocity his flesh had become, pustulant, taut, brimming with the aching energy of the Abyss seeking to enter this world, the world of blood and bone. Five pairs of eyes watched his excruciating transformation. The five nameless whores, whom he had filled with seed before slitting their throats, five offerings in a foolish gambit he never truly understood. And now they were undead midwives, impatiently awaiting the coming birth.

Millis had spent many nights prowling the downtown streets of nearby cities and towns, posting ads online, and lingering in kinky chat rooms, looking for Jodie Foster lookalikes. When he had the five he needed, the five called for in the damned fraudulent spell, he brought them, one at a time, to a cheap, musty motel on Rte 128. He gave them heroin, pills, and Absolut vodka, and let them play their heavy metal ballads or their hardcore gangsta rap as they danced and stumbled on the dingy bed in the glaring headlights from the nearby highway.

They had all been so beautiful, these lost girls with hollow eyes, even when he broke their necks.

They drooled black fluid now, carelessly stumbling over their spilled innards, a syrupy mess that muddied their slow, circular progression around him. They spoke, these Jodies, but not any words Millis understood. They coughed out harsh syllables marred by the thick, clotting blood that filled their rotting throats. Prayers or curses, who could say?

Their rotting was attractive in its own way, as is the cloying death of a rose after weeks of bloom. And the five Jodies clearly still had some siren allure from their sidewalk days, for throughout the long, aching, sunless hours imprisoned in the abandoned station, Millis watched as homeless men and runaway teenagers made their way, somehow, down into the depths, drawn by some primal need. He watched as the men disrobed and silently embraced the rotting hookers and allowed themselves to be torn open by broken glass bottles, teeth, and fingernails, and then the hunger would rise inside him until it burned, and no matter how much he tried to fight it, he would feast on the hot muscle, the lungs and the heart, and gulp down the salty liquor of their fading life.

And inside him, inside his massive womb, a fanged thing already jerked with abandon, frantic for its release. He was freezing cold one instant, then molten hot the next, only to plunge again into cold. His swollen abdomen, pale and immense, beggared reason, nestled as it was in a pile of entrails and offal that roiled with the shiver of maggots and the buzzing wings of blood-fattened flies.

And then, with little in the way of warning, Roger Millis began to give birth.

A hooked talon poked through the skin of his stomach. It looked like a carbonized nail. Another joined it, and they grasped the edge of the rent and pulled, stretching both the skein of reality and his sweat-sheened skin. It tore at both, eager to be born, pulling itself from the gelid, congealed amnion of the eternal Abyss into the warm fetor of the subway station. Ribs cracked and bone shattered as the demon burst from the wound, from the ruin that was his lower body, but miraculously Millis lived. He was both witness and mother, the explosive ruin of his lower torso left him mute, a macabre mermaid: part man, part bloody ruination.

Millis could only stare in awe as the blood-misted demon stretched to its full height, flexed its newly incarnated muscles, and roared as it sprayed vast torrents of meconium into the shadows.

He had been such a fool. This was no simple demon or flibbertigibbet to be hex-driven into mortal service, no dim-witted succubus to be coaxed to orgasm with coins or promises. This was Giblis, birthed in the darkness before the stars, servant of the eternal Abyss.

Millis was fading fast, no amount of blood or magic could sustain him. He wanted to speak, to ask for forgiveness, but could only cough out blood as he died.

The demon Giblis sidled close to the corpse of its summoner and mother, confused.

It was supposed to be the one known as Stromm, but that betrayer had forgotten his allegiance to the Abyss. Released into the world, Stromm had been seduced by the powers of the flesh and mind. He had forgotten his true self. He had refused to stage another summoning to free Giblis from where he had been bound.

It was strange, though. If it weren't for this corpse at his feet, Giblis would still be imprisoned. How was it that this one could have called him forth? This simple man? The air still tingled with the vestiges of the amateur's warding spell. These were cantrips taught to schoolboys. This one should not have had the knowledge to free him. Surveying the area, it became clear that the man had not known much of anything, least of all the ways of the Abyss.

The demon grinned. This man had been a puppet, then. There was another player in the game, someone who wanted Giblis free to play a role in his schemes. This stranger would soon learn that demons are not playthings. Giblis would bow to no man, and he was not going to return to the Abyss. Not this time.

No, he would make of this world a throne.

The demon caught something on the air, something very faint, but painful. The cloying scent of burnt poppies. Absinthe. The moist stink of desperation, patchouli, sweaty sex. Cordite. There were trinkets scattered around the circle, each tainted with the scent of a man. Giblis recognized the smells, and his face split with a grin. His jailer was involved. He would have his vengeance at last.

The massive demon whirled, mindlessly shattering the spine of one of the Jodies with his serrated tail. He roared, shaking the tracks. "Grange!"

Four dead prostitutes screamed with malodorous joy as they danced around the demon. The remaining Jodie, broken by its carelessness, pulled her shattered self forward to lick and caress the demon's still-smoldering skin.

"I don't understand why you unleashed him."

"The demon?" said Cascade. "Or Hiram Grange?"

"You do seem to be at cross purposes."

"A test, then, General. Steel must be tempered. The Abyss and the earth have their own champions. They both have their uses. This will determine which is the more suitable for our plans."

"This is very dangerous."

"Most undertakings of any worth usually are, no?"

"You are gambling with the fate of the world."

Cascade laughed. "Worlds, old friend. Worlds."

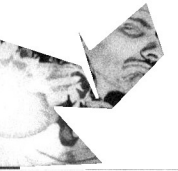

Hiram Grange crouched in the deepening snow, peering at the entrance to Mindware Research Facility #9 though the perimeter fence. According to the information Hiram had been given, the Facility had been closed just a week ago after a recent Life for All protest had become violent and several students had been killed. Plans were already in motion to demolish the building and create a memorial park. Clever corporate politics to smooth over the negative publicity.

He had put in a call to the Office for more details, but they had little beyond the basic facts gleaned from a quick Internet search. The rumors concerned something called the Digital Eucharist, some new technology that Mindware had recently perfected and was preparing to distribute. The rumors also claimed it was why the company was taken over by the Movement. Jeremiah Stromm had wanted the technology for himself.

Well, it was now or never. Salt crunched underfoot as Hiram darted across the long stretch of shoveled driveway. He reached a steel door and pressed himself against the wall beside it. Saying a prayer to the green fairy, he swiped the stolen key card, feeling a tension release inside him when the light turned green with a click. Pulling the door open, he slipped inside the darkened building, where there was glorious, wondrous, majestic heat.

To Hiram, the future always smelled like dried blood and smeared shit and biting antiseptic cleansers. The future smelled like the blue, biting tang of electrical burns and scorched blood. The future—so bright, shiny, and new—all too often smelled like death.

With all that he had seen, Hiram didn't really trust science, not much further than the chemical cataclysm that propelled a bullet through the throat of his Webley, or the perfect mesmerism of alcohol and smooth hallucinogenics and opiates that enshrouded him for the briefest of moments from the harshness of the outside world. No, it would not be accurate to say Hiram disliked science, but he was fearful of it. Just as those undisciplined students of the darkest occult arts were likely to unleash a scaly madness beyond their control, a scientist intent only on the promise of the future may find some new atom to split or some new virus to unleash. Hiram knew enough about human nature to know that, in some small way, Oppenheimer's blood must have quickened when Hiroshima bloomed, and it was likely that his manhood swelled along with the mushroom cloud.

Much could be forgiven in the name of science. The ends always justified the means. Injecting rats with wild, coiled viruses and then popping off their tiny elongated skulls to see their brains swell as they careened through cardboard mazes trailing streams of frightened piss. Drilling holes in the craniums of dolphins and piercing the pale brain matter with serrated electrodes, then pushing a button that makes them shit and piss and chew on their tongues. It was all neatly documented in Moleskine notebooks, this clever science. Here and there a bloody thumbprint would mar the edge of a page filled with tight, scrawled penmanship.

Hiram Grange had seen much working for the Office, had witnessed plenty of strange stuff on his many excursions for Bothwell. But whether it was a pale corpse spit forth from an enchanted grave, or crazy clones, or an intelligent plasma that prophesied for the military, there was always a danger of going too far, of crossing some invisible line that, once broken, could never be restored. What was the world like before fire? Before the wheel? Before gunpowder? What was it like before man, and all his dreams of progress?

The research facility was a disaster. Spray-painted slogans dripped on the walls. Buckets of pigs' blood had been splashed across oriental carpets. Desktop PCs, laptops, and server towers had all been ransacked, their sides torn open, their hard drives removed, leaving just the frayed edges of cables and power cords visible. Monitors were overturned, many on the floor, their screens shattered. A metallic case was splayed open against the wall, shards of broken glass canisters spread around it. Several puddles of a dark, purplish syrup, filled with fragments of jagged silver, stained the carpet.

Hiram examined the case. There were ten cushioned sockets inside. Nine were empty, one was occupied by an intact glass canister. It was labeled with a sticker: Digital Eucharist, Batch #75309. The canister contained a bluish liquid that was slightly more viscous than water. A quicksilver globule pooled at the bottom.

It seemed to sense his presence and shifted slowly. Suddenly, it spit forth spines tipped with hooks. It tapped at the glass with each spine. Hiram placed his hand against the glass and the globule grew more frantic, each barbed protrusion rapidly tapping against the glass where his hand had warmed it. It resembled a maniacal metal sea urchin. The clicking became more fierce and insistent, vibrating the canister. For a moment Hiram was certain that the vessel would shatter under the assault.

Hiram quickly set the canister down and the quicksilver urchin's mania seemed to subside; it settled back into its senescent, ovoid shape.

Hiram slipped the canister into his pocket. Bothwell's techs would love to get their hands on it.

At first Hiram found it hard to believe that people would willingly ingest the Digital Eucharist, but the more he thought about it the more it seemed commonplace, inevitable. Kids split their tongues or pierced their eyelids to impress the girl next door; others embedded microchips in their fingertips because they were too lazy to carry a set of car keys. It was clear that any new technological advancement would lead to people clamoring for more ways to meld their bodies with the latest shiny gadget. Cochlear implants. Bionic eyes. Subdermal implants. Sexual tech. Technology was a slope lubed with K-Y Jelly.

The Digital Eucharist. It sounded so perfect. A way to be truly connected with others who thought the same way you did, to share their very thoughts and feelings, to know the deepest secrets of their souls. It would beat the piss out of an iPhone any day. Hiram could see the appeal.

The disheveled offices opened to a hallway that led to an unlit laboratory.

Hiram's hand dropped to the certainty of his Webley. He felt a tingling along his neck, that feeling of being watched, an atavistic feeling of being preyed upon. It was something ancient at the base of his brain being tickled by the animal scents filling the air.

He was definitely being watched.

As Hiram stepped into the laboratory, shards of broken glass grated under his brogues. There was a thin whining sound off in the distance. His shoes began to stick as they would to the floor of a movie theater or one of those sour private booths where you press your face against a cold metal viewer and rub yourself raw to decades-old footage of naughty teens now six feet underground, but here in the laboratory the darkness was absolute and what gripped his shoes could only be blood.

His outstretched hands brushed against the cold, thin metal bars of cages. The whining sound increased until there was a loud pop, and a momentary burst of blue light from a shattered electrical outlet cast the room into bright relief for the barest of seconds—a flash of lightning, but its passing served only to blind Hiram further. The darkness was now sour velvet.

Something moved in the blackness as though shifting from one foot to another. Hiram pressed himself against the wall and gripped the trigger of the Webley. The gun felt good and solid. For a long, strange moment, the gun was the only thing that felt real, and everything around him seemed vaporous and sinking, and it seemed to Hiram that the blood-soaked floors would dissolve away and drop him into emptiness. Gods, he needed another pill, something spiky and bright. He needed a drink.

Hiram stepped into the room beyond, holding his breath to listen for anything behind him. After a count of ten, he let his hand slide across the wall until it found the cold metal plate of a light switch. Running his fingers over the switch, he flipped it.

Long fluorescent bulbs in the ceiling brought themselves to life, throwing off a pale light.

Thirty dead, emaciated chimpanzees stared back at him with cloudy eyes.

The diapered chimps were strapped to stainless steel X-shaped frames, their arms and legs spread wide, electrified metal collars holding their necks in place. Shaved scalps had been peeled away

and the craniums sawed off just above the eyes. Hiram expected to see wires piercing the brain meat or thick cords jacked into chrome boxes bolted to the skull.

This was different. A thin lace of wire mesh had grown throughout each simian brain. The metal glinted wherever it poked through the meat, the filaments forming intricate loops, spirals, and elaborate designs. The chimps had been wired from the inside out with a nanotech lace. This was the Digital Eucharist laid bare. Liquid webware. A neural lace that overruns the brain, burrowing into the cortex and the lobes. Subdermal routers. The Occlusionists were using this to link their members together, to make them one gestalt organism.

No, that was not right. The Digital Eucharist was about control. This was the invisible leash that held its myriad members in check. Stromm was the one who held that leash. This was not good at all.

The whining returned, a wail of pent-up electricity. The fluorescent tubes dimmed overhead, grew perilously bright, and then one by one they shattered until only a single bulb remained, casting its light in a steady throbbing that pulsed in time with his heart.

The room erupted with primal screams.

The crucified chimps rattled their steel frames, and their jaws worked furiously. Black snot oozed from their noses, and yellowish gobs of lung butter hung from their dry, cracked lips. Their eyes fixed on Hiram, unblinking, sixty white orbs glowing with a hungry, delirious insanity. A dark energy coursed through them now. The wire lace filling their brains began to glow orange. The sizzling, smoking brain meat gave off the smell of a greasy diner, filling the room with thick, oily smoke. Jaws began to snap shut slowly, and then with more violence, until the beasts were stretching their maws insanely wide and slamming them shut, cracking teeth and tearing dead tongues with every bite.

A chimpanzee managed to free an arm by breaking it at the wrist and tearing the dried flesh away. The bony stump flailed wildly as it locked its eyes on Hiram, blackened lips cracking and splitting as they were pulled into a bloody smile. Its fur erupted into flame from a molten brainpan, the fire rapidly spreading, leaping from one simian to the next.

The flaming chimps began to speak.

"*Hir.*"

"*Am.*"

They each took a turn speaking a syllable, the air filling with the sour rot of their decaying lungs.

"*I.*"

Wet, sour coughs.

"*I,*" croaked another. "*Am.*"

One blew a bubble of black snot. "*I. Am. Free.*"

And then the unseen hand that had resurrected the chimpanzees unleashed the full potential of the sinister current that gave them a cruel semblance of life. The air throbbed with the spent energy. The thirty simian brains glowed molten red, and then one by one the sizzling skulls burst, splattering hot bits of brain into Hiram's face, into his eyes.

A scalding gobbet of brain matter landed on Hiram's lips, filling his mouth with its vile taste.

Hiram was caught between screaming and laughing.

The same thing had happened when his mother shot herself.

iram gathered himself just as he heard shouted voices. He wasn't sure if it was the police or security, but he needed to get out of here. Hiram found a flight of stairs and quickly climbed to the second floor, thinking as fast as he could. He checked the hallway before slipping into a maintenance closet. The room was tiny, filled with mops and the biting scent of bleach, illuminated only by moonlight beaming through a small window. Hiram tried to force the window open, but it refused to move. It was either painted shut or frozen in place. Voices moved up the hallway.

He tried the window again, slamming his palm against the frame, once, twice, until finally it inched forward with a clatter of ice on the sill. Icicles shattered and rained down. He caught his breath, certain he'd been heard, but after a minute the voices seemed to fade away. He shoved again and opened the window wide enough to fit his lanky frame through. The cold night air filled his lungs.

Hiram balanced on three stacked boxes of cleansers and pushed himself forward, arching his body up as he shimmied through the window. He had little leverage but needed to reach the roof, which was a few feet above the window. Standing on the precarious sill, he was just able to reach a rain gutter. The cold metal burned his bare hands, but he couldn't let go. With one foot, he nudged the window closed. They would probably notice the arctic chill in the room and figure out where Hiram had gone, but it might give him the precious seconds he needed to escape.

He pulled himself up onto the roof, cursing the bitter New England winter, Bothwell and her smug imperiousness, and the distinct lack of absinthe in his bloodstream.

Just as he caught his breath, Hiram saw multiple vehicles pulling up in front of the building, joining the one that was already parked. Headlights glared along the walls of nearby buildings. Hiram crouched and ran to the edge of the roof, peering over. Three black vans were parked in a semicircle at the front, their side doors open. Three teams of four men each had exited the van, brandishing semiautomatics. They all wore matching winter military gear with a patch above the right breast of each, an open white eye. It seemed the Occlusionist Movement had a private security force. Curiouser and curiouser.

A long guy-wire spanned the expanse between this building and a small garage fifteen yards away. Hiram tested it and prayed to Kali's left breast that it would hold.

Slipping the glass canister into his coat, he grasped the cold wire with both hands, kicking up and wrapping his spindly legs around it. Spidering out gingerly across the span between the two buildings, he resisted the urge to look down, ignoring the burning pain of the frosty cable. He would have traded his liver for a pair of insulated gloves. Voices sounded from somewhere below, but luckily no one had rounded the corner of the building yet. He would be too exposed

Inside his jacket the canister began to vibrate. His body warmth must have awakened the Digital Eucharist. Hiram imagined the silver thing shattering the glass and piercing his stomach with its spines, burrowing into him, and feeding with abandon.

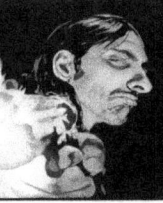

Chapter Eight

Hiram knew there were too many coincidences, too many truths that he had failed to see. That he had not allowed himself to see. This was a trap. The levers and the gears were artfully concealed, but Hiram could sense them grinding away. He was being set up for something he couldn't see, but he knew it now, and knowing allowed him the chance to avoid it. Or to dive right into it with the Webley spitting vengeance.

He had to go underground.

He had to see that the confluence was still sealed. Needed to see for himself that the demon Giblis was still bound in the Abyss.

Because if it was free, then everything would change.

As he walked past, Hiram could see that the Occlusionist Tower was sealed off. The broken windows had been replaced, and armed guards were stationed around the front entrance. They were taking no chances with protesters, or meddling secret agents, for that matter. A few people managed to enter the Tower, but as Hiram watched them pass through metal detectors and biometric scanners, it became increasingly clear that the only way into the Tower now was with the Digital Eucharist. Only those truly trusted, those wired to the Movement, would be let through the doors.

He would need to figure something out.

Aside from the Occlusionist Tower, Boston's downtown area had undergone some major renovations in the years since Hiram had first come here. The Combat Zone, with its neon-blinking sex shops, smoke-filled peep shows, and $10 whores with needle-bit arms, had been swept away and replaced by theaters, condominiums, and posh boutiques. Hiram wasn't sure the change was all that different, or any better. It was merely a bandage over a festering wound, and the quality of the band-aid could do little to stem the slow, certain rise of pus and stinking odor of sickness that rose from cold, sterile streets.

Even though it had been years, he still knew the way underground.

He descended the escalator at the Downtown Crossing station and passed through the turnstiles to the platform. After an outbound train passed and the platform was emptied of riders, Hiram jumped down, keeping a careful eye on the third rail, and ran for a hundred yards along the tracks. Crushed, soot-covered stone grated under his feet. Several times, Hiram caught the quick movements of blackened rats fleeing at the sound of his footfalls. The ground began to vibrate as a train approached, its running lights illuminating the tunnel walls.

Hiram managed to reach a service nook just in time, and he was forced to wait several long seconds, his back pressed against cold stone, as the train rushed past, the warm air of the city's exhalation roaring in his face. After the train had gone, he ran again until he found an unlocked service entrance that allowed him into a utility hallway running parallel with the outbound track. Several flights of concrete stairs brought him deeper into the earth. Four levels down, he was forced to break the rusted lock on a steel door before entering into a warren of abandoned offices and storage rooms, the air thick with the fungal scent of wet papers. All of the ceiling lights were shattered or shorted out. In the glare of his flashlight he often came across signs that humans had once camped here: trash, spray-painted epithets, makeshift altars; either foolish college fraternity pranks or homeless or shattered folks seeking solace in the depths of the city.

Despite the darkness and the labyrinthine corridors, Hiram moved with singular purpose, something inside him guiding his step. He knew exactly where he was heading. The flashlight revealed the broken glass that crunched underfoot, and the walls were shiny with dripping, oily water. At last Hiram reached the door he recognized. The rusted handle came off in his hand, so he shouldered it open and made his way onto the West platform of the abandoned station.

The Downtown Mission station had always been associated with violence and murder, if only at first due to the fact that two popular crime movies had been filmed there in the late '40s. But it was the five long months of public outcry following the Abyss Murders in 1969 that ultimately forced the politicians to close the entire station, seal it off with cement, and reroute the tracks.

On a wintry Monday morning, subway conductor Donnie Pace had stopped his three-car Red Line train just shy of the platform. As he began speaking in tongues over the intercom, his brothers, Roger, Keith, and Jaybo, each in their chosen car, reached into their knapsacks and started tossing grenades and gas canisters. In a span of mere minutes, they killed 138 people, along with themselves, filling the underground station with meaty black smoke and vicious flames. Donnie Pace had opened his own throat with a razor blade.

Horrific as the event was, several elements helped raise it to an international story. Among the victims was Melissa Tyce, a stunning ingénue infamous in Hollywood for servicing the members of the Rat Pack—all at the same time; legendary jazz man Hammer White; Percival Winters, the wealthy financier and art collector; and the entire second grade class of Sewell-Anderson Grade School, who had been in town to ride on the Swan Boats.

What lit the fuse beneath the public's outrage, though, was surely the matriarch of the Pace family, Maureen Pace—Crazy Mo, as the neighborhood kids called her. Standing before a crowd of reporters and four television cameras, Mrs. Pace insisted that her sons had always been good boys, and the sorry business with the train, well ... that was merely the work of the Lord. She then lunged forward and bit the nose off of a reporter, chewed it with relish, and swallowed.

She had then turned to the news cameras and revealed a bloody-toothed grin.

"Welcome to the Abyss," she said.

Those were the last words she ever spoke.

Years later, Hiram Grange had helped prevent a trio of demons from using the weakened skein of reality in the subway station to escape the Abyss, and nearly lost his soul in the process. It had ended badly. Very badly. A woman had died. Hiram had killed her. And now it seemed that it had never really ended at all. She was dead for nothing.

Here Hiram was again. He had hoped he was wrong, but somehow knew that he wasn't. Now, there was no longer any doubt.

The smells that assailed Hiram answered his questions immediately. Rotting meat, the biting scent of smoldering hair, blood—all too clearly redolent of the ashen scent of the Abyss. Across the platform, he saw the teeming pile of white, roiling maggots and the lashing tails of soot-darkened rats. Hopping onto the tracks, Hiram made his way across to the other platform, dancing over the third rail, although this stretch of track should have been inert for decades. He could leave nothing to chance now.

His hand reached for his holster and found the metal comfort of his Webley. Hiram had filled the five chambers with demon shot, bullets throated with mercury and white gold dust. The sixth chamber held the suicide shell, empty of powder or shot, yet filled with everything that mattered to him.

The reptilian stench told him he'd been wise to find those bullets.

Hiram pulled himself up onto the platform and warily approached the birthing pile. Pulling a long flare from his satchel, he cracked it open. Its bright orange glow illuminated the underground chamber. He tossed it into the mound of carrion eaters. The rats scurried away, but the maggots remained, sizzling in their idiot greed. In the shifting red light, Hiram could see the fragments of body parts, human and otherwise, and the white splinters of broken bone. A pile of livers and hearts was set off to one side, corrupting in the heat. Fragments of a warding circle were hidden now beneath the spreading slime of corruption, the eldritch energies long since faded from the sigils and precise lines.

Another fucking group of Seven, or maybe someone else entirely, had undone the bindings that held Giblis in the Abyss, that kept him and his kind away from this world they despised and wanted to devour.

Hiram felt something inside himself come undone. Knowing the demon was free released a fierce tension he hadn't even known was there. The empty malaise with which he idly walked the streets of the city was now filled with the certainty of what he would be facing. It steeled him, gave him a solid purpose. It

made his trigger finger itch. This time he wouldn't banish the demon back to the Abyss. Not again.

He was going to destroy the very memory of the fucking scaly beast named Giblis. For her. For her memory, at least. Not for forgiveness, but for salvation.

A set of large, clawed footprints led away from the mess of blood and innards. But Hiram didn't need to follow them. He knew in his soul where Giblis had gone. It was all too clear now. The demon would be drawn to the opening microconfluences in the Occlusionist Tower; those momentary glimpses of the Abyss would be like catnip for the demon.

Hiram saw it then. Some madman had devised this. The pieces had been carefully put into place and the plan set in motion. Was Stromm behind this entire thing? Somehow that didn't feel right to Hiram. Someone wanted Hiram and the demon to meet again. But why?

He would have to get into the Tower again to find out. He thought he might have a way.

Hiram felt the hairs on his neck rise. He felt exposed, as though he were in the crosshairs of a rifle scope or his scent was on some fanged serpent's tongue. Something predatory was watching from the shadows, he was sure. Planting his feet, he slowly eased the Webley from its holster, cocking the hammer back. He stepped gingerly over the mess before him, trying to find a suitable place that would offer some means of defense, some wall to put his back against. He eased the Pritchard bayonet into place on the barrel of the pistol.

A broken thing burst from the shadows, screaming. A shattered corpse with the angelic face of his dreams. Hiram froze in disbelief. Jodie Foster? She pulled herself across the cement with ruined hands, trailing lengths of dusty, ragged intestine behind. The bones of her shattered spine scraped on the cement, vertebrae dangling from long threads of tissue. She grasped onto Hiram's legs with frozen hands and started to pull herself up, a puppy overjoyed to see its master; only this horrid thing was delirious with insatiable hunger, clawing and snapping at him.

The hot, sour stench of death punched into Hiram, stinging his eyes and making him gag. He kicked her away and raised the Webley. Through the cheap makeup and rot, he could see that she was merely a pale imitation of Jodie, circa her role in *Panic Room*, and nothing like the profound glory of the real thing. Hiram calmly fired a shot directly into the pitiful creature's skull. She fell to the platform with a wet slap, her split skull oozing a porridge of rotted brain matter.

The explosion echoed in the abandoned subway, and Hiram's ears rang with the violence of it. The pleasing smoke of cordite hid the charnel stink for a moment, and Hiram sucked it in greedily, inhaling the memory of the gunshot.

He began to shake then, the reality of it all slamming home. He needed his pipe and his blessed Presbyterian Mixture. He needed a drink; he needed to really drink.

He needed a moment of normalcy before he pursued the demon.

He needed someone warm.

Gnashing teeth and clawing would be just fine, just as long as she was warm.

Hiram awoke from dreamless oblivion to the smell of burnt things. The tang of caramelized sugar filled the air. A few sugar cubes were still piled next to an empty bottle of absinthe, the green lady drained down to her last delirious drop. A syringe lay next to a charred spoon, bent like a dead insect, reeking of tar. Crushed remnants of clove cigarettes filled the ashtray, along with a few crumpled condom wrappers.

The nameless woman he had taken back to the Airstream was gone. So was his wallet. But all that didn't matter in the light of day.

Giblis was free. The Occlusionist Movement had to be some sort of elaborate cover to free the demon. Hiram didn't know how, but it was all tied together. The bastard Stromm had somehow returned from the Abyss and had now finished what he'd started long ago, bringing a demon into the world.

Hiram was terrified, but knew he would have to face the demon again. There was no choice.

The empty absinthe bottle mocked him. His baggie was now only dusted with the remnants of his precious opium. He did manage to find a few pills and capsules scattered on the carpet, mixed with some aspirin tablets. Scooping them all together, he popped them into his mouth. He needed something to wash them down. Praying to the nine billion names of god that there was a beer left, Hiram opened the small fridge to see three bottles remaining in a four-pack of wine coolers. Little Miss Nameless must have left them behind. Hiram cursed.

Sunshine Berry flavor.

The universe was a malevolent bitch.

At least they were screw tops.

Hiram needed to steel himself, prepare for the coming confrontation. He had defeated the demon once before, but wasn't sure he was willing to pay that horrific cost again. As he sipped at the vile malt beverage and chewed the pills, Hiram remembered back to that night, far beneath the city, when everything had gone to hell.

The binding circle had been broken, wiped away by the sneaky demon's urine, and Giblis was breaking free.

The demon's hand darted out through the break in the circle, grabbed Laveaux by the shoulder, and pulled him in. Giblis hammered a blow against the man's rib cage, cracking several ribs and dropping him to his knees. The demon's talons bit into Laveaux's shoulder as he was pulled off the ground, his legs dangling. Giblis spread his bestial jaws. The inside of its mouth was impossibly red and crowded with cruel white teeth. It leaned in and snapped its mouth shut on Laveaux's left thigh, then shook its head violently back and forth as it ground the bloody flesh from the bone, crunching the femur to pulpy shards. Giblis tossed the screaming Laveaux away.

The broken circle's energies were spent, but the demon was still bound to its confines. That would only last for a few minutes more. Soon it would be free.

"*Stay back!*"

Elise fired two shots into the demon, but it shrugged them off.

A taloned hand darted out, grabbed her, and yanked her into the circle. Elise screamed as Giblis pressed her against its smoldering body. Her skin blistered from the heat. The pain made her pass out.

Sprawled on the ground, Laveaux managed to fire off one shot before blood loss weakened him and made him drop his gun. The shot went wide, shattering some decayed brick. He set off a flaming cantrip at the end of his stump, cauterizing the wound with a blinding flash. The air filled with oily, black smoke and the coppery stench of burned steaks.

Hiram quickly reloaded his Webley with a speed-loader and fired off five shots. He kept pulling the trigger after the fifth, but there was just the empty click of the hammer striking spent shells. It didn't matter anyway. Demons were immune to mere lead.

Giblis still held tightly to Elise, now mercifully unconscious of her plight.

Soon the circle would be gone entirely.

Giblis laughed. *"I can smell your fear. Hiram, is it? Five bullets? Why?"*

Hiram froze. He felt the demon inside his head, burrowing through his thoughts. It knew his name.

The demon started laughing. *"Your mother. You carry the memories of your mother around in your little gun. What would Freud say to that?"*

There was one last speed-loader in his pouch, but Hiram couldn't move. He felt as a small bird might when faced with the perfect, mesmerizing eyes of a serpent. Something primal at the base of his skull held him immobile.

"*We know your mother well in the Abyss,*" Giblis said, laughing. "*So very well. Sadie, too. We know them all.*"

Lies, Hiram knew. Foul lies. But they still cut like razors. Pierced him to his core.

"Don't listen to it," rasped Laveaux. He was covered in sweat, fighting to remain conscious. "Don't listen."

Hiram had only seconds, and then the demon would be upon him.

He turned and started from the chamber.

"*Run, Hiram Grange! I still will find you.*" The demon mocked him.

Hiram stopped. Everything stopped. There was only his breathing now. Only his breath. He turned and faced the demon. He walked toward it, careful step by step. He saw nothing. Only his breath.

"*Perhaps if you kneel, Grange, I will be merciful.*"

Hiram nodded.

"You bastard!" Laveaux cursed him.

Hiram reached into his pouch, ignoring the reloader. He let the Webley slip from his right hand. His other hand still searching, he knelt and dropped his head.

The demon's laughter intensified. It was a cruel, mocking sound.

Hiram's fingers found what they were looking for. Molded from the grease of roasted swans mixed with the dust of crushed barnacles and ink from gigantic albino squid, the grease chalk was an essential carrier of the binding spell's energies. Hiram withdrew the black chalk stick and slashed it wildly back and forth across the floor before him, roaring his defiance to the world.

"*Hiram!*" Laveaux screamed. "*No!*"

The demon wailed, realization dawning in its alien mind.

With a final swipe of the chalk, the binding circle was closed again. It was misshapen, surely, but puissant nonetheless. The energies of the binding spell increased in power now, dancing around the completed circle in blinding blue light, throwing biting sparks and searing bolts inward to lash the insane, howling demon.

And to lash the beautiful girl it still held prisoner in its arms.

The horrendous pain must have awakened her. Elise lifted her head weakly, lost and confused, and her eyes caught Hiram's just as he finished the spell to reseal the confluence. Her hair caught fire.

"Close," Hiram whispered.

"*No!*" It was a cry Hiram would never forget, for it was a cry formed of many voices. The bereft Laveaux losing his love; the demon Giblis, defeated and enraged; and Elise, who lost everything there was to lose.

The black chalk flared like the sun, the fierce, cold energies of the Abyss fighting mightily against the young, vibrant magicks of the binding spell. The letters and sigils flashed themselves onto Hiram's retinas, and he was thrown back by the force of the closing confluence. The entire underground chamber was thrown into darkness, a blackness to match the emptiness that was growing inside him.

iram had relived that moment hundreds of times since, and now the demon he'd sacrificed so much to imprison was free again. He had killed Elise for nothing.

Hiram had no absinthe or whiskey or pills left to obscure the pain, except for one thing. It was dangerous, a wild risk, but he had nothing left to lose. He needed to get into the Tower. Elise would be avenged.

He picked up the small wooden box with intricate scrollwork on its lid that Laveaux had given him. Laveaux had called it the Scorpion's Kiss.

Hiram crushed some of the leaves and mixed it with the powder. Packing his pipe, he ignited it and inhaled deeply. Almost immediately, his fingers and toes began to tingle. A pleasing warmth started at the base of his spine and spiraled upward. He took some more, sucking the bowl to ashes. He was numb.

Hiram put the pipe on the table and picked up the glass canister he had recovered from the abandoned laboratory. He unscrewed the cap.

The Digital Eucharist lurked at the bottom, writhing like a ball of silver eels. The canister shifted with the weight of its twisting and turning. It seemed to sense his intent, growing eager with each passing second. Hiram pressed the edge of the canister against his wide lips and let a few splashes of the cool suspension liquid hit the tip of his tongue.

The silvery mass leaped up, piercing the meat of his tongue and gums, pulling itself into his mouth. It felt like he had swallowed a thousand fishhooks. The restless thing buzzed with insistent energy, shooting out spiked, superfine tendrils in every direction, pulling itself inside him. It tore into his sublingual vein and dosed him with a soporific akin to the finest Thai opium.

The mass then split itself in two. One half forced itself down his throat and into arterial streams, trailing antennae lengths of warm, vibrating thread. The remaining half split again and wormed its way up each eustachian tube, narrowing and then swelling when they reached the mastoid emptiness behind each ear. The Digital Eucharist truly bloomed into a flower of relentless agony, burrowing eager slivers into the meat of his brain with steel ferocity.

Reality began to fade.

Aside from the wild ringing in his ears and the warm, medicinal stupor that filled his limbs with warm cotton, the Digital Eucharist affected his vision first. Everything around him shone with brightness, a clarity that was not there before, and Hiram saw flickers of things behind reality, the solidity of ancient bone and steel beneath the everyday world.

Hiram sat still for many moments as the voices began, first one, then a thousand, until his mind was filled with legions of voices, all calling out to him. Through this all was the demanding voice of Stromm, urging his followers to come to the Tower, to protect him against those who sought to overthrow the Throne of Vision.

The stone around his neck vibrated. Hiram hoped the drugs coursing through his system would be enough to hold the Digital Eucharist at bay, at least for as long as he needed to gain access to the Tower.

Hiram found he was able to reach out and become part of the multitude, sharing their thoughts, their sights. Through countless eyes, Hiram saw the Occlusionist Tower rising from the masses crowded around it. The windows glowed a sickening red, each like the eye of an enraged demon.

Giblis had already entered the Tower.

War had begun.

The Occlusionist Tower rose from the crowds surrounding it. Its windows throbbed a malevolent red. Faces were rendered into stark masks of longing, of emptiness, waiting for something, anything. These were the mindless drones of the Digital Eucharist, drawn to the Tower by the hungry, insane power controlling their minds. They clogged the streets for several blocks around.

Hiram moved slowly through the crowd, ignored by everyone. Those around him stood slack-jawed, murmuring a single syllable, as though they all shared one mind. The assemblage felt like some vast organism, hydra-headed, their upturned faces bloodied by the radiant crimson light shining from windows of the Occlusionist Tower.

Careless of the bitter cold, many were dressed just in their nightclothes, a few were nude and shivering blue. Several police cars were parked at the edges of the crowd, their lights flashing. Some of the officers stood apart, warily monitoring the strange crowd, while others, linked to the Eucharist, eagerly became part of the growing throng.

The Digital Eucharist clearly had been distributed far and wide, burrowed into the unsuspecting brains of thousands, patiently waiting for the moment when their hidden master had need of them.

The demon Giblis, however, was usurping the Occlusionist Movement's plans.

Nobody stopped Hiram as he moved forward. They could

sense his Digital Eucharist, recognized him as one of their own. Hiram knew how tenuous his presence here was; were they to realize what he was, who he was, they would slaughter him and bathe in his blood, for none could approach the Tower that was not clean and perfect and chosen.

Hiram was none of those things.

The soft sibilance of the Digital Eucharist called to Hiram, trying to seduce him and gain control. He managed to keep it at bay, barely. The insane mix of drugs buzzing through his system somehow prevented it from taking over. It seemed as though the closer he moved toward the Tower, however, the more the Eucharist's signal increased. The nanotech lace in his brain longed to connect to the true source. Hiram felt its quicksilver shifting inside him, icy worms dancing beneath his flesh, as it sought the correct configuration that would bind him to the Movement. Soon his mind would not be his own.

Hiram walked up to the front door and stood for a moment while invisible eyes, both electronic and eldritch, scanned him. Locks clicked, the glass doors hissed open, and he entered the large, opulent lobby. It appeared empty, but the sweet scent of decaying flesh filled the air, and wet, oily footprints showed where a dark thing had been prowling. Hiram followed the footsteps to a huddled shadow in the corner; it stood and shambled toward him.

"*Hiram*," it said. The dead Jodie Foster managed only that one word before her decaying jaw fell off. She limped toward him, another dark parody of all Jodie had ever been. Blood spilled from her nostrils, bubbling with dark energies. This young zombie was the spitting image of Jodie from *Taxi Driver*; even beneath the decaying skin, Hiram saw the glorious resemblance.

She even wore the same clothes, that perfect flowered shirt. Her body's corrupt fluids now stained it, though, and the smell nearly overwhelmed him, a tangible odor that threatened to reach into his throat and pull out his stomach.

Hiram had an instinct to press pause and rewind, as he always did when Jodie came on the screen, but this was real. This was happening. It was madness!

He was surprised to see the Webley already in his hand and raised; as though it had a mind of its own. He hesitated. Hiram hated himself for it, but something in this rotten, shambling thing spoke to his darker self, something about it excited him. He watched her take another step, wanting her to be closer, just a little bit closer. Cursing, he pulled the trigger and a bullet pierced her skull, followed quickly by another. She fell to the ground with a sigh.

He quickly reloaded, knowing there would be more to come, as behind him the elevator pinged and the *Up* arrow glowed. The doors spread open, unleashing the foulest scent of the grave that Hiram had ever encountered. The miasma was visible, a green, gaseous cloud that shimmered with Abyssal energies. He nearly fell to his knees.

Out of the luminescent stench, Clarice Starling, Sarah Tobias, and Erica Bain lurched forward, each a rotting effigy of his perfect, delicious, most angelic Jodie.

Hiram froze. It wasn't the dead Jodies that horrified him, though. Not entirely. It was his exposed secret. Only Sadie knew. No, only Sadie had known. Now someone else also knew his darkest secret, and was exploiting it, taunting him with it. Someone knew the depths of his soul and was revealing it to the entire world.

What other secrets were known? Was everything about him to be revealed?

Hiram stood still as the Jodies grabbed him and pulled him down.

Their skin felt damp and rough. When they pressed against his body, he felt the cold jelly of their dissolution. Skin tore and flesh gave way as cheeks, lips, and scalps sloughed off in rancid clumps to reveal gleaming bone. They teemed with voracious mites, these goddesses, and maggots bubbled in their wounded throats. Pale fanged things, borne of the Abyss, nestled restlessly in their desiccated wombs. The three Jodies bit and clawed at him, tore at his clothes. That darkness that lurked inside him, that small, shameful sliver, welcomed this apotheosis of all his fantasies.

Jodie, in all her rarest forms: Sarah Tobias, the rape victim from *The Accused*, pinned him down, soaking him with her sour, clotted spillage; the cold, impenetrable FBI Agent Clarice Starling from *Silence of the Lambs* peeled the pale breasts from her chest and offered the dripping lumps of meat to him; the taut, steely Erica Bain from *The Brave One* knelt beside him, her meat-soaked breath hot on his neck.

"He made us. For you. He made you. For us."

Blood hammered in Hiram's veins. His head pounded.

For a brief moment, he wanted to lay back and let them take him, to derive some small solace from the death they were to deliver, to become some eldritch saint that is made holy as he is eaten and ingested and subsumed by others.

The part of him that wanted to die lost out to the part that wanted redemption. To make himself worthy of what Sadie had seen in him. The fire of rage ignited again inside. His hand wrapped around the comfortable handle of the Webley. He shot the Jodie that straddled him, exploding her belly in a sticky cloud of black blood. She dropped off, still jabbering, until he fired into her face. A third shot brought Clarice Starling down; he fired another shot out of pique that his favorite version of Jodie had been so defiled. He emptied the Webley on the last, pathetic version of Jodie Foster, and, despite it all, he did shed a tear as she fell.

He breathed in the silent, cordite-scented air. The smoke from his Webley and the corruption from the undead Jodies became all too much, and Hiram vomited, sicking up wine coolers and pills.

He reloaded the Webley once again, then took the wooden box out of his pocket and emptied the contents into his mouth, chewing the bitter mixture and mixing it with his saliva. He pounded the elevator button, and the doors spread open, but this time the elevator car was empty. The carpet was slick with foul, necrotic juices. Stepping inside, he scanned the keypad. The hidden circuitry of the security system pinged his neural ware and several more numbers illuminated. His cracked connection to the Digital Eucharist gave him access to the entire building, but Hiram only cared about one destination: the fortieth floor of the Occlusionist Tower, where Stromm and the demon Giblis waited.

The top of the Tower was where he was going to kill the demon, or die trying. Maybe both. He was too tired to care beyond that.

This bank of elevators only reached the halfway mark; he would need to change on the twentieth floor. He pressed the button and began a smooth, rapid ascent.

Chapter Eleven

Hiram counted the floors as the lights ticked them off. He actually grew calmer as the numbers rose. The opiates and hallucinogens in the Scorpion's Kiss filled him with a tranquil madness. It would all be over soon, one way or another.

There was a violent lurch in his vision, and for a brief moment Hiram was seeing the chaos through Stromm's eyes, several floors above. Something dark and reptilian was pursuing him, destroying everything in its path, leaving blood and gore in its wake. Hiram's heart pounded in sympathy with Stromm's. That primordial fear the man was feeling must have been shared across the entire Movement, by every single drone bound up in the thrall of the Digital Eucharist. The demon roared and Stromm screamed. It seared like a molten knife through Hiram's cortex.

The Scorpion's Kiss began to flower now, and it warred with the technology of the Digital Eucharist, each demanding control over his thoughts. His ego was shattered, pulled apart, and put together again in perverse, perfect ways. Everything around him shimmered. The elevator seemed to be moving sideways now, shrinking and expanding like a beating heart. He saw the elevator walls peel away to reveal metal supports, cables, and wiring, until those also faded to reveal stars and pure darkness. He saw through the veils of reality. It took a long moment to realize that he was looking into the Abyss itself, pulsing just beyond the earthly realm.

It had been years since Hiram had first seen the Abyss,

had first seen into the gulf of cold emptiness and malice that threatened the world with cold annihilation.

Hiram stood still, feeling the throbbing energies just beneath the surface of reality, like the pulsing of a thick, meaty artery filled with starlight. It made his teeth ache. The Abyss was incomprehensibly vast. Countless horrors and unknowable minds occasionally peeled back the layers between realities and greedily poked their wild, blood-soaked eyes into our world, and sometimes they managed to slip themselves through, the lords of appetite, to devour mankind and his dreams.

For a brief moment, Hiram felt everything shift, and it seemed he was standing inside the Abyss, and everything of the world he had known was now distant and cold—as if every memory he knew from his childhood and the deafening shot that felled his mother and the years of drug-fueled sex and mayhem and Goth music and gunfire, gunfire, gunfire—everything was born of the empty, galactic cold that was the Abyss; and beyond the veils, through them, was the true warmth, the everlasting warmth, that was blood and was kisses and was life and was her name, what was her name? That girl, that goddess, that one he had seen through the mirror. Jodie? No. Sadie? No. Hiram shivered, certain he would shatter.

One night, soon after finishing school, and before this life had truly begun, he had taken the finest opium, and a half bottle of Johnnie Walker Blue, and several red pills, more yellows, and tiny tabs of paper with smiley faces on them laced with LSD, and there were smoking candles made from the tallow of crippled cows and tinny-sounding, mind-bending music eked from an old cassette player. Was he kneeling amongst the insects at Angkor Wat or standing nude at sunset at Machu Picchu or holding his breath as he swam amongst the ashes of ancestors in the Ganges? Among all the colors, red tells the most lies. Had he been sitting on his parents' bed in his abandoned ancestral home? Time is shaped like a scorpion.

He saw so much darkness on that drug-fueled trip, so many dumpsters in his mind had been upended and overturned and the contents set aflame. What does suicide taste like? Hiram had seen a glimmer of light in the Abyss, too. He had seen something that burned inside him to this day. He had seen beauty. Not the flesh-stiffening kind of lustful want, but the beauty that broke your bones and made you new. It was what he had seen in Sadie's eyes.

Hiram searched for it now, yearned for it, among the colossal stones and frozen wastes that filled his vision. Math does not work here; language is impossible. His eyes were designed to see light and shadow, the mere reflections of true reality, but that had all fallen away. He was seeing truth. His desires were generative, libidinal; his want, his need, took the stuff of creation and made.

There was the faintest glimmer at first, and then she came into focus, nameless but known. Details were impossible to discern and retain, shifting as they did with every fierce beat of his heart. There were wings, surely, but two or two million, Hiram couldn't say. Colors faded into the purity of absence, starlight was shrouded in leagues of gossamer silks of pink and yellow and green and fire.

Cities encrusted her eyelids, those blue-tinted orbs luminous and warm, a raging fire in these cold places. The benevolence in those eyes could only be maternal, though what planetary beasts spilled from her cavernous womb surely beggared reason. She was hunched over in the vast darkness, imprisoned perhaps, forgotten by most, besieged by ages, a mountain that slept and dreamed of waking.

Somehow, beyond all reason, the mere speck of Hiram's presence in the Abyss—his mind, his body, he did not know—aroused her, and her immensity shifted, glacially slow, but with an authority that astounded him. She shook off eons of dust as she unfolded multifaceted limbs, unwinding muscles and ligaments, and her shining globose eyes blinked, casting down nations, as she stretched forth a hand toward him, her fingers five forested peninsulas, then five immense, gnarled trees, then five carved bones of elder beasts, and then five soft digits of a newborn child pressing warmly against the skin of Hiram's chest.

Her fingers had been stone, the bones of ancient continents, and now they were softness itself, alive and warm. They awakened something inside him, something that had slept since Sadie's death. The fingers now blazed, scarring him. The heat filled his entire body with peace and with an increasing pain. The sizzling meaty smell of cooked flesh and the black oily smoke of rendering fat filled his nose.

Something was wrong. His vision filled with a moment of static, an antique radio blared nonsense in his ears.

This wasn't real. This was illusion. The truth was a lie.

The cooking flesh was his own; the agony engulfing him was the Digital Eucharist seeking final control over his mind. The lodestone burned in its pouch around his neck.

Then the reality of it all slammed into him. A microconfluence was opening inside his mind. No amount of drugs could stave off the technology forever. That tenuous joining of flesh and spirit inside him was being severed, making way for the Digital Eucharist and its mechanical wants and needs, filling his veins with limitless opium and peace, freeing him from this world of sweat and toil and sadness, preparing him for the welcoming arms of Jodie.

Jodie. It would be so easy to give in, wouldn't it?

Did he not deserve happiness, too? Jodie.

Just relax and let sleep come. Give in, it whispered.

Sadie. Poor, sad Sadie. Death.

The pleasing warmth of the Digital Eucharist now became stifling, raging with an unchecked heat. Hiram started to struggle, clawing his way from the mindless stupor he'd been trapped inside, trying to awaken himself. He was miles beneath the surface of icy, black water, unsure of which way to swim toward the solace of fresh air. His entire being screamed with the lack of oxygen. There was the violent scent of lilacs.

"Fight it, Grange," a woman's voice shouted. Sadie? *"Or I'll slice your throat myself."*

A flaming spike pierced Hiram's chest and filled his heart with the fire of a thousand suns. He looked down and the shining spear that glowed from the throbbing wound became a compressed hypodermic syringe. Adrenaline. Hiram tore at the smoking lodestone scalding his chest and threw it to the floor. His shirt still smoldered; his scorched chest was red and swollen.

The elevator doors were open. He had reached the twentieth floor. An android geisha was pulling him from the elevator into pure, bloody chaos. Several men and women, drones all, were holding their heads, screaming. Android geishas seemed to be on a rampage, lashing out at anyone around them. A few functioned normally, and when they saw Hiram, the intruder, they advanced.

After pushing Hiram to the side, the android geisha raised its hand. It held his Webley. Before Hiram could react, it fired over his shoulder into the face of a wild-eyed drone that had come up behind him. The flash scalded his cheek.

The back of the drone's head exploded in a red spray.

"Grange, you can use this relic better than I." The android tossed the gun to him, and then lashed out at another drone with a fierce kick, knocking him across the room. The android reached up and ripped off its faceplate to reveal a face Hiram had seen before. The animal rights protester that had dragged him from the lobby. But he had seen her before that, too, now that he saw her features clearly. Always a quick glimpse in crowds, disappearing whenever he turned, fragments of wild dreams that faded all too quickly in the light of day, always a warm, pleasing fragrance of lilacs. Was she following him? She had to be. Who was she? Her face was hard, beautiful, but he did not know her.

A silver knife flashed in her hands as she leapt onto a table. She was bleeding profusely from her side. She had brought him back from the edge of the Abyss, jabbing that needle into his heart. What was she doing here? Who did she work for?

"There are no innocents here, Grange," she said. "They are all too far gone. Use your bullets well." She leapt from the table toward two androids, piercing the chest of one with her knife and shouldering the other to the ground. She stepped onto the elevator and slammed the *Down* button. Her hand went to the wound in her side. "I can do no more here." The doors closed and she was gone.

Hiram resisted the urge to go after her, to ask her who she was, why she was following him. All around him, the androids continued their mad assault. But these were not androids at all, he realized; they were failed experiments, early test subjects of the Digital Eucharist. Without orders, they were aimless drones lashing out in terror. But they were still dangerous.

Hiram ran to the executive bank of elevators with a fury, fighting his way through the gauntlet of androids. They were living, breathing humans beneath the carved steel masks, but their minds had long been given over to the Movement. A few had torn their masks off to reveal pallid, scarred faces beneath. Electrodes pierced their craniums; their tongues had been cut out. Their eyes were wide with misery, and Hiram liked to think he saw pleading in them. He saw every shot of the Webley as a mercy killing; putting down a foam-slathered rabid dog was no less cruel, no less necessary.

The Digital Eucharist struggled to gain control of his mind again, but the insane mix of drugs was helping to keep it at bay. The adrenaline that raced through him was a godsend. He felt invincible.

The Webley emptied just as he reached the elevator to the top floor. It was open, waiting patiently it seemed for him. He stepped inside and welcomed the silence as the doors hissed closed and the car began to rise.

Only then did he notice that he was out of bullets.

His experiences with the Digital Eucharist made Hiram realize that this had nothing to do with the teachings of some New Age cult. It had a much darker purpose. The Digital Eucharist didn't just create microconfluences; it was designed to communicate through them.

It all snapped into place. Hiram's imagination filled with a battalion of soldiers: gifted with the Digital Eucharist, e-trained with centuries of martial tactics and enhanced with the latest techno-flesh augmentations, and totally under control and obedient to generals in hidden bunkers. There was no battlefield they would not dominate on this world. Or on any other. Hiram was stunned by the monstrosity of the plan. Soldiers wired with the Digital Eucharist could be sent anywhere—they could be sent *through confluences*—and still they would be under the control their master.

This was not a war of flesh and blood, though there would be plenty of that to be sure. This was a war of the mind and the imagination.

No, the Digital Eucharist was not designed for religions or cults. It was designed for something more profound, something more outrageous.

It was designed to mount an invasion of the Abyss.

The elevator stopped and the doors opened to silence.

The adrenaline was fire inside him; everything was so crisp. Hiram had never moved with such certainty of purpose. For the barest of moments, he could feel the suicide shell somehow adding an odd heft to the empty gun in his hand, as though it was akin to the heart of a star, but its strange, empowering gravity was the weight of memory, of regret. He had so many sins to atone for, so many failures that he carried in that chamber.

Sadie. Elise. So many things he had to answer for.

A short distance down the darkened hallway, past a row of antique statues, was the Inner Sanctum. Hiram pushed at the open door with his foot. Large monitors filled one wall. Some showed the empty lobby and several floors filled with mayhem, others were tuned to multiple feeds and newscasts from around the world. Smaller screens flashed metronomic gatherings of letters that flickered at the very edge of comprehension: *Be Peace. The Closed Eye Sees More. Truth Is False. Become Free. Tomorrow Is Now.*

The Throne of Vision was like something out of a science

fiction film, a large chair beneath an organic-looking metallic crown sprouting wires in a thick, braided cord. The cord unraveled as it approached an array of consoles and panels covering the walls, each individual wire jacking into slots and outlets and inputs.

Jeremiah Stromm sat hunched down in the Throne, his white suit disheveled, blood spreading from a shoulder wound. His breathing was labored.

A strong reptilian taint soured the air.

"He said I would be the one," Stromm mumbled. "Cascade said I would be protected, that I would be saved." The old man seemed to be laughing, but from madness or glee, it was hard to say. "I was supposed to rule."

An immense figure rose up behind the man, nearly blotting out the light from the monitors. A large hand with thorn-like claws wrapped around Stromm's throat and jerked him out of the Throne. Moving from the shadows, the feral red eyes of Giblis pierced Hiram. A smile filled the demon's face. Stromm's legs kicked frantically, but the demon treated the man as an annoying gnat, nothing more.

"*I knew we would face one another again, Hiram Grange,*" said Giblis. "*It was the sole thought that preserved my mind within the Abyss, which kept me from fading into the anonymous mass.*

"*This Stromm vessel was supposed to prepare the way for my return. But he became greedy. He tried to delay my summoning and keep power for himself. His kind always do.*" Its massive hand clenched around Stromm's neck and jerked, cracking the man's spine.

Giblis extended a talon and poked it into Stromm's throat, worrying the point deeper and deeper. The demon slashed the

razor-sharp talon downward, opening the old man from throat to navel to reveal a shining worm-like creature nestled among the intricately carved bones, clockwork gears, and rough iron of the remade Stromm. The High Adept of the Seven had been reborn in the Abyss, hollowed out and rebuilt as a puppet.

Giblis grasped the keening worm and slipped its chattering head into his mouth, gnashing it to glimmering shreds in his teeth. The demon let Stromm's limp, bloody skin-suit flop to the floor. *"Corpse riders are never to be trusted."*

Hiram raised the Webley, his hand shaking.

Giblis laughed, deep and guttural. It spread its arms wide, almost as a welcoming gesture. *"The gun is empty, Grange. I have been watching your progress. Your mother's bullet is all that you have left. Such a tasty irony, no?"*

Without thought, Hiram reached for the Pritchard bayonet and slid it into place on the Webley. He ran forward, aiming for what he hoped was the demon's heart. Giblis swiped an arm across, grasping Hiram's wrist, knocking the gun from his hand, then yanked Hiram forward, nearly wrenching his arm from the socket. The demon's tail whipped around and slammed against Hiram's legs, knocking them out from under him, shattering bone.

The pain in Hiram's right leg nearly caused him to black out. Jagged points of bone pierced his bloody pant leg. Any movement threatened a loss of consciousness.

"I have spent endless hours in the Abyss thinking of all the ways I would break you, trickster, but I see now that with this device I can ruin your entire world. I can fulfill the promise of my birth by making it ready for the Archons."

Hiram could only watch in silence as Giblis worried his enormous bulk into the Vision Throne. The crown looked obscene on the demon's head, insectile and robotic at the same time.

The air above the Throne was filled with the scintillating energies of the device, the demon's malicious thoughts made visible, throbbing and bloody. Hiram could barely imagine the levels of malice that would be broadcast into the minds of those linked to the Digital Eucharist, the wild, frothing abandon of chaos and mayhem that would be unleashed.

Hiram could almost hear the screams as unwitting drones reached up to claw their own eyes from their sockets, or as mothers took their smiling infants and dashed their skulls onto the concrete pavement. There would be countless thousands of small atrocities, murders and suicides, rapes and other mindless violent acts, all single notes feeding into a symphony of terror that would never cease, for even those unlinked would be affected. Planes would fall from the sky or be carefully guided to oblivion. Highways would run with blood. Hunters would find darker prey, turning their guns on loved ones and then themselves. Mothers would grind their infants' fingers between their teeth. Hiram shuddered to think that somewhere a drone's hand could be hovering over a red button, *The* Button, waiting patiently, so eagerly, for the Word from the Throne.

The Webley was nearby, but Hiram cursed it. There were no more bullets. He had no more speed-loaders. The Pritchard had snapped off and was now nowhere in sight.

Hiram's eyes dropped and focused on the large transformer that led to the Vision Throne; it already buzzed at capacity. Giblis was learning to use the device, contacting those infected with the Digital Eucharist technology, slowly reaching his vile thoughts out into the world. Hiram took a deep breath and pulled himself across the floor, slowly, maddeningly, the agony in his leg incredible. The adrenaline had worn off, and his muscles buzzed with exhaustion.

An edge of exposed bone caught on the carpet and Hiram nearly screamed aloud.

Giblis ignored him. Its reptilian form was slouched back in the Throne, its eyes turned back in its head, flickering. It was one with the machine.

Hiram raised the Webley. For a brief moment, he dared to hope the empty chamber would be filled, with a miracle perhaps, with a dream, with something to stop this monstrous being from shredding everything that was worth saving in the world. He pulled the trigger, praying for cataclysm, but there was just the empty click of the hammer striking neutered brass.

Hiram turned his gun, kissed it, and gripped it by the barrel. He slammed the butt down on the transformer as hard as he could. Again. He struck several times in rapid succession until the gun, his faithful Webley, came undone in his hand, the metal pieces falling to the carpet. Five empty chambers gaped at him. The suicide shell mocked him with its impotence. The demon growled deep in its throat, intent on its increasing control of millions of minds, its bestial maw spread with an idiot grin.

Hiram started pounding on the transformer with his fists, heedless of his own pain. He knew it was pointless, though. He had done all that he could. He had failed. Again.

Defeated, Hiram struck again in frustration and winced as his hand came away trailing blood. He stared at the blood pouring from his palm, dazed.

He had cracked the casing of the transformer. A thin rent in the metal exposed wires, solenoids, and coiled copper cylinders. He stared at the opening for a long time, his mind nearly empty.

At last, Hiram forced himself up onto his knees; his leg burned with the flames of an infinite hell, but he refused to feel the pain any longer. He was done with it. He shuffled forward, unzipped his pants, and unfurled himself. It took forever, but at last he forced himself to release a meager stream of piss, darkening the rug as the arc increased, leaning forward, there, just enough to splash onto the cracked casing and start seeping inside; moisture, ions, and sodium, and sparks, please more sparks, more delicious, delightful, wondrous sparks, dimming lights, and Hiram laughing, giggling, insane with exhaustion and agony and terror about what he had failed to stop, and him pissing the last ounce of his energies away.

There was a deafening pop, and then several staccato bursts of light. A thick, deep buzzing rose and fell with the strength of the lights. The energies above the Throne were chaotic. The demon opened its reddened eyes, groggy with the euphoria of its dominance. A lightning storm erupted from the transformer, energies loudly coiling up the wire and sparking across the metal tips of the crown like St. Elmo's fire, blue and purple, actinic and bright.

The moist scent of scorched reptilian meat filled the room. Giblis roared as the six tendrils of the crown tensed up, grinding into its massive skull. A violent surge of electricity forced the crown to slam shut, piercing its skull in six places, carving its head like a well-sliced fruit. The crown's metal points met in the center of the demon's brain, arced and ignited a tiny, brief, efficient sun to wipe away the darkness.

Hiram was still laughing when he lapsed into unconsciousness.

"So, the entire operation was a fiasco."

"Was it?"

"It is just that I thought the Mindware technology would be useful to us."

"It will be. We have all the research and records that we need. And we know it will work in the way we want."

"What if Grange had failed?"

"There are contingencies for everything, General. Sometimes towers fall."

"And what of those infected with the Digital Eucharist technology?"

"It will have burned itself out when the Vision Throne was destroyed. A fail-safe built into the nanotech."

"Some will be lost without their tech. There may be questions."

"I doubt it, General. Increased violent impulses, limited critical or rational thought, blind obedience to trends and fads. Do me a favor, will you? Turn on the nearest newscast and you tell me if anyone will ever notice the difference."

"Damn, Grange, you really should lose some weight. We make quite de pair. Two working legs between us."

Hiram was sprawled on his back, watching ceiling tiles slide by. He was on a wooden serving dolly being pushed by Bale Laveaux. He wasn't quite sure where he was. Laveaux was perched on the edge of the dolly, using his one leg to propel them down the hall toward the elevator. Sweat already covered his face.

"Where is my tie?" Hiram said. His father's suit was a sorry mess. The pieces of the Webley had been stuffed in the coat pockets. "Hey, why is my fly undone?"

Laveaux shook his head, whistling. "That is between you and your demon.

"Called Gertz and he is on the way. Said he would get word to Bothwell. There is going to be a hornet's nest outside after this."

"What the hell are you doing here?"

Laveaux laughed. "Sometimes Papa Ghede says no, you hear? I realized that when someone offers you everything you want, you should run the other way."

Hiram had no idea what Bale was talking about, and the pain spiking through his leg made it all too easy to ignore.

"It wasn't that hard to find you. The *loas* know your name, Grange. They led me to this building. The androids and those zombies all fell once you did whatever it is that you did. People are puking up quicksilver and blood all over the place."

"Thanks for coming after me," Grange said. "I'm surprised."

"You didn't kill her, Grange," said Laveaux. His face was blank for a moment. "A demon did. And the thing about demons is sometimes dey wear white."

"I owe you one, Laveaux," Hiram said.

"We ain't ever going to be friends, Grange. But if we meet again, let it be as strangers meet."

The elevator whirred to life and Hiram felt that gentle shift in his innards as it plunged toward the ground. He hoped Bothwell was waiting with an ambulance full of meds. He hoped the nurses were libertines and barely legal. He hoped there was some whiskey, and maybe a wee bit of opium.

He hoped for ... well, he hoped. And that was enough for now.

BONUS SHORT STORY

Bruise for Bruise

by

Robert Davies

This story first appeared in Weird Tales *#353*

J oss Coffington came to Promise to find the girl with God on her back.

He had heard many rumors about the strange town before, and had passed along a few he had made up when he was on his sixth or seventh beer, but it wasn't until he heard that particular rumor, that of the bruised girl, that he finally took to walking. He wasn't alone on those dusty back roads either, and most of them that crowded Joss on the road were going to see the girl, too, going to the town of Promise, where monsters were born.

Some said it was contaminated well water or rainbow glinting oils that shimmered on the creek, drowned ill spirits or chemicals that spurred the blood to strange, unseen designs. Others claimed it was unseen radiation pulsing from the new power lines that snaked across the sky, trailing alongside the highway between here and there. Still others said it was simply divine will made flesh, a harsh judgment made upon a town founded by sinners when the country was being born. Perhaps it was without any reason at all, but each passing year saw strange folk filling the small houses and narrow roads of Promise, united only by their differences, untouched by the world beyond.

The birth rate in Promise was low—snake-belly low to be

precise. Whether the fault lay in the seed or in the womb, none could say; but, in those jackpot moments when life found root, the town of Promise could be sure of one thing: after nine months of morning sickness and sibilant prayer, something never seen before would be spilled screaming into the world, or silent as the case may be.

Sometimes there would be something of the mother in the child, and sometimes something of the father; there was always something of the town. Leathery wings sprouted oftentimes, as common as fingers. Fur of every hue. Horns and scales were plentiful, too. Lots of feathers and thorns and glass and steel. Beneath the apple trees and the pine, anatomy was negotiable. Anything was probable. Every now and then, though, the tired wet nurses, long inured to the strange fecundity of flesh, would whistle in awe as they lifted a newborn from the amniotic slime.

Something truly special would be seen.

The Eddington triplets were each born with an extra mouth on their foreheads; the better to sing His praises, Father Quine had said, smiling. Justice Peck arrived, took two deep breaths, and burst into silent blue flame. The great-granddaughter of Old Khoas was born flower-faced and her every breath was a yellow cloud of pollen. Jirrup the Younger emerged limbless and scaled, and like the original beast his eyes were eyes of gold. The blind watchmaker's daughter Undulia grew monstrously fat and fetid as she approached her blessed day. She spilled her blue-eyed daughter in a ruinous, thick tide. To the shock of all, this newborn daughter, grunting and wailing, then gave birth to another smaller girl the size of a fist, swollen with child. This last tiny daughter, still nameless, still shivering with the chill outside the womb, stood shakily and birthed a finger-sized son whose wormy penis dragged on the floor.

Ruth's twin brothers, Luke and Persistence, came into the world in a crimson flood, the jagged steel knives growing out of their fingers and cruelly hooked thumbs must have sorely treated their mother's insides. She had survived, though it had been doubtful considering the blood that had come that December morning, and it was this improbable survival that made her someone of consequence in the town, with handsome Father Quine singling her out as a model of right living and righteous prayer.

Ruth Mingleton, however, seemed plainer than milk when she came two years later. Excitement and congratulations for a healthy girl quickly gave way to uneasy smiles and averted eyes, until soon the townsfolk were crossing the street to avoid the Mingletons and their enigmatic child. Ruth was one of the untouched, it seemed—a curiosity in a town of curiosities.

Ruth's father was let go from the sawmill; later that week, he was let down from the wobbling rafters of their ancient barn, his pants filled and his throat maroon. Her two brothers, her mother and Ruth kept to themselves then, the pale blue curtains drawn, the doors bolted. They seldom ventured into the town save for the Sunday sermons of Father Quine, though they sat at the very back, and for the necessary staples of whiskey, gossip, and salt. They helped keep the glass smith in business, so it seemed, as their windows were often shattered by stones; the perilous, unkempt lawn in front of their house came to glitter in the moonlight.

They lived like that for years until Luke and Persistence snuck away one night and got themselves hitched to the passing Carnival of Blood and Thunder that was keen on upgrading its freak show. But too much cheap whisky, an aversion to cayenne, and too many fistfights over the insatiable and mercurial

Lobster Girl finally got them fired on the outskirts of Biloxi in a thunderstorm, and they came back to the town, heartbroken, penniless, and sullen as ever.

And so the story has it that it came in the darkest part of night, with a hammer and with nails and with hands that wielded them with a feral mastery. Down through the ceiling, or up through the floor, one could not rightly say. It came upon Ruth on the eve of her thirteenth birthday and made her anew. It found the bruises beneath her skin and made of them a poetry. It found the songs in her bones and made them break. It found the angel she saw on the tain and ruined its pale and perfect skin.

Ruth Mingleton didn't even cry.

She awoke to find bluish yellow smears spread across her skin—an image of a thorn on her cheek, a suggestion of velvet wings on her stomach, a golden hint of the lip-stained Grail on her inner thigh. The bones beneath her skin only accentuated the designs: her breathing would give flight to a seabird on her right shoulder, the shift of her jaw would rock the ark on her throat.

It was Ruth's mother that brought the bruises to the attention of Father Quine.

Dressed in the perfect fuligin of faith, Meticulous Quine sported great, snowy wings, just like ancient Uriel of the Scarred Palms. His black eyes glinted, and his voice was honey. He saw something in the bruises that most others did not. Ruth's mother saw it, too. They prayed together.

The townsfolk quickly took interest in Ruth then, began to murmur that she had finally revealed the gift of her birth. Of course, many claimed they had known all along that Ruth was special, revealing the hidden bits of wisdom they had hoarded for years, awaiting this day of revelation. Others, mostly those left-handed it must be said, still expressed doubt, but they were quickly silenced by the knowing frowns of Father Quine or the squinting glare of Ruth's mother. Ruth's brothers would shake their glinting fingers and make them ring.

The bruises began to change with time, the soft canvas of her flesh revealing some new wonder nearly every other day. A bruised serpent coiled around her leg. Lazarus awoke on her forehead in shades of blue and black. Her bruised flesh revealed the world as it was before we fell, her belly marred with the aching greens of an Eden gone awry, her palm marked with a bruised piece of silver. And those places that wouldn't bruise, like her tongue, inexplicably bled.

The excitement in the town waned rather quickly, however, what with the coming of the harvest and the promise of another deep, implacable winter.

It was then that the breathtaking bruise of the thrice-nailed Christ across her back appeared. While the lesser transgressions on Ruth's arms and legs quickly healed, the Christ refused to fade. Indeed, He seemed to gain solidity with every passing day, and the stony dust of Golgotha circling her waist sprouted pale yellow flowers that glistened when she sweat.

The townsfolk crowded the narrow lane to the Mingleton's house from sunrise to dark, pleading for a chance to see, perhaps to touch, whispering and pointing out those that had thrown stones or foolishly spoken ill words before.

The pilgrims came soon after.

They came first from the outlying tobacco farms and corn fields, and then neighboring towns and fishing villages, and then from those distant states where truth can be a crime. Some carried the heavy riches they had acquired, eager to lay them before Ruth;

others came with only scraps of cloth wrapping their bloody feet and foreign tongues in their mouths. One and all they came for the daughter of bruises and the stories on her skin.

Father Quine and the town elders ordered a scaffold and stage of rough-hewn wood to be erected on the Common, on the very spot where a meteorite fell in the time before trees. Blood-red tents quickly sprung up around the scaffold, followed by hawkers' tables and kiosks and craft-laden blankets until the entire common resembled a harvest fair. Meaty smoke rose from hissing, snapping cooking fires. Brightly colored pennons snapped. They built the ticket booth on the distant edge of the Common. To lessen the taint of commerce around such a profound miracle, Father Quine had said. Great lengths of yellow rope were strung up to form an orderly queue, snaking back and forth across the trampled grass.

Luke and Persistence collected the golden tickets at the foot of the stairs at the side of the stage, spearing them with their jagged fingers. At the ticket booth, Ruth's mother counted the money, each coin like a rosary bead in her calloused hands. Father Quine passed through the crowds nibbling on sugared insects, looking about with unconcealed pride, his wings stirring the warm, summer air.

Ruth sat on a stool at the center of the stage, a flask of warm water by her feet. She wore denim shorts and a thin white shirt that barely covered her tiny breasts. It was ripped open in the back, the better to reveal the bruised face and chest of the crucified Christ.

Nobody ever asked, but the bruises did hurt her. Each new one ached to the very heart of the bone. Sometimes Ruth awoke with a cracked rib, her breath piercing like a knife. Sometimes she awoke only to faint away from the nauseous pain writhing beneath her skin. Still, she would sit patiently on her stool as the sunburned pilgrims bought their tickets, formed a line, and ascended the stairs to examine her flesh. Lesser, smaller bruises appeared daily on her wrists and throat, her feet and her belly, her breasts, but the pilgrims hardly noticed these scenes from forgotten pages of the Bible and those other books.

They had come only for the Christ.

At the end of the day, Ruth's mother would climb the stairs and lead her back home, Luke and Persistence following a few steps back. Ruth always trembled as she walked, her legs grown stiff, her stomach empty. A few of the more pious pilgrims would trail behind the Mingletons and gather in small groups outside their house; some took to picking up the shards of glass that still littered the lawn, placing them on the tongue and swallowing them. But all the curtains were drawn tight, and in time the darkness and the silence would urge the pilgrims to move on.

Her mother examined Ruth every evening, her calloused hands flexing as she traced the fading lines of bruises and injured flesh. She marked which bruises were fading, and which were still visible. When she was done, truly done, she sent Ruth to stumble onto her mattress. Ruth slept, but she never dreamed.

After two weeks on the stage, Ruth hardly saw the pilgrims anymore as they passed before her. The pain of her new bruises and splintered bone paled beneath the simple, dull ache of sitting there, pilgrim by pilgrim, hour upon hour, sunrise until sunset. The sun burned her skin. Insects bit her eyelids and buzzed in her ears. Through it all, her bruises shone with vitality, in strange, curious shapes that beguiled the eye.

So, of course, Ruth did not notice when Joss Coffington stopped before her, and she did not hear when he stifled a cry.

Only after several moments did she realize he stood there at all, his shadow shielding her from the blinding sun. He did not look at her wounds; he was looking at her face, at her.

"I love you," he said. He stood there, unmoving. Ruth looked up and caught a glimpse of his face before he was ushered off the stage by the stern-faced Father Quine.

Ruth was not so complacent after that. She started to look at the pilgrims as they came to see her, looking into their faces for something, making some uncomfortable, making some regret. Father Quine suggested a hood, and her mother agreed; but a few days later a crown of thorny bruises circled Ruth's brow, with glinting red berries of blood, and the hood was forgotten and the ticket price was raised.

Joss Coffington returned, day after day, ignoring the dark looks of Father Quine and Ruth's mother, ignoring the increasing cost as they tried to dissuade him. He paid whatever they asked and climbed the stair to stand before her, shielding her from the hot sun, if only for a moment. Most days he said nothing. On others, he again professed his love for her. Sometimes he smiled, but it seemed quite difficult for him to do. He always stood until he was forced off the platform by Father Quine or one of Ruth's brothers.

So it came to pass that on one of those August days that made you curse the sun, Ruth waited on the stool, ignoring the countless pilgrims that passed by her and their pleas for healing or riches or prophecy. She was blind with agony, sweating. A large bruise on her right leg showed the epic Fall of Jericho; the whisper of angels casting down that ancient wall had nearly broken the femur in three places, so fierce was the reckoning of their angelic fury.

It was late in the day, and he had not yet come. She feared

they had finally scared him off. Her mouth was dry but she did not care any longer. She almost let herself slip from the stool, let herself slip from her skin.

Father Quine's voice broke the silence, and a scuffle broke out in the line. Ruth turned to see Joss Coffington push Quine and a few pilgrims aside and dart up the stairs.

He ran to her and put his hand on her shoulder.

"You don't have to stay here," he said.

He reached down and pulled her arm, but she was immovable, inviolate in her agony. A statue would have moved more readily; but where a statue would be cool stone, she was fevered, damp flesh. She looked into his eyes.

"Go," she said. "Go, before it is too late."

Footsteps rattled the scaffold. Persistence and Luke moved forward as one. Father Quine urged them on. Persistence grabbed Joss Coffington by the collar and pulled him down, his fingers slicing into Coffington's shoulders. Luke slammed his right knee into Coffington's face with a wet crack, again and again. Persistence kicked his spine and slashed at his side. Coffington fell limp.

The crowd barely reacted. If anything, they regarded the entire event as an inconvenience, something that kept them from the momentary miracle of standing before Ruth and seeing her bruises and her pain. They had all come so far to see her. They had waited so long.

Ruth saw Joss Coffington lying on the scaffold. She sat still. Her hands opened and closed.

A silence fell on the crowd.

Ruth seemed to whisper to herself, looking down.

"What is it, child?" said Father Quine.

She whispered again.

Father Quine moved to her side, leaning down to hear.

Striking like a cobra, Ruth grabbed Father Quine's arm and he dropped to his knees. The memory of her every wound passed through her fingertips and burned into his mind. His skin grew damp and darkened with Biblical scenes. Bone snapped and feathers smoked. Reddish spittle fell from his mouth, followed by a scream. Father Quine slumped forward, his wings aflame.

Ruth stood and looked toward her brothers. "Stand back," she said, her fingertips smoldering. "I have ages within me."

Persistence and Luke stood still, shocked by her feral eyes. But their surprise gave way and as one they smiled and slowly circled her like hungry wolves. Their mother shouted from the chaotic crowd. People pushed and shoved to get out of the way, their eyes fixated on the strange tableau upon the stage. Those wise to the danger of crowds drifted away from the stage, forking their fingers and spitting twice.

The brothers lunged, but they were thrown back

Thrown back not by force, but by a look, a casual gesture. Each jerked upright, like fish upon the line, held in place by unseen chains. Dark, bruised lines slipped across their faces, across the skin of their throats; the painful lines formed angels, magi, and flibbertigibbets by the dozen. Reptilian in their speed, they shifted so quickly that it seemed the figures danced. The skin split in their wake, bleeding. The lines slowed and dissipated, leaving the brothers' sweat-sheeted skin red. Spent, they dropped to the platform, one atop the other.

Ruth's dripping hands were ruined now, tattered and charred.

She knelt beside Joss Coffington and touched his face. She listened at his mouth for breath. Her shattered fingers trailed across his chest and found no heartbeat.

She turned to face the crowd, and her eyes held only vengeance. Not the petty vengeance of rage or jealousy, but that primordial ire that ignited the stars. Ruth found her mother and pointed directly at her, freezing her in place. Ruth's gaze took in the entire crowd, each one a celebrant, each one an idolater. Ruth shouted a word heard only in the quiet days before the caul dried on the world, and she tore her throat to shreds.

Everyone in the town felt it, though none would ever agree what had happened.

Some said it was a simple feather or the passing of warm wind over a cloudy dandelion; others said it was the touch of a lover, of a mother, of a glass-eyed stranger. Some said it felt like grass growing. Others mentioned razors, warm oil, and the cracking of a knuckle. Old Khoas said it was rust, and he was right. A few said nothing at all, but it was there in their eyes. It entered them, unfurled itself, and never left.

She opened Joss Coffington's shirt and pressed her smoldering hand against his chest. The blood spilling from her mouth sizzled when it hit her fingers. She leaned against him, putting all her weight against that hand. Her shirt fell away, and her bruises were lambent.

There was that strange wind again and Ruth stood, her eyes wild.

Joss Coffington sat up and winced. He looked up and took Ruth's waiting hand.

The mark of her hand on his chest had swollen already, the skin shiny and red. What she did to the townsfolk that day, she did to him, too, only different. Everything they were, the secrets of their blood and memories, was now in him, coiled like so many serpents, all clenched at the base of his skull like a writhing fist. He was legion.

She put an arm around him and they walked off the stage and down the stairs, heedless of the crowds around them. A few of the townsfolk knelt, reaching out to touch them as they passed. One brushed a finger against the gaping wound at Coffington's side, pulling it away with awe.

They walked out of the town, and they walked until their feet bled, and then they walked until the stars filled the sky. Those that followed after Joss and Ruth lost them in the darkness in a matter of hours. None saw them after that.

Behind them, in Promise, it took several weeks for the stories and rumors to die down. The townsfolk tried to carry on as they had before, but something was amiss. Old Khoas was the first to notice, but he said nothing. The wooden platform fell during a bad nor'easter and the town was suffocated in white. The frightened elders called a meeting on the town common and patiently waited as everyone came. The blue moonlight blackening their faces, the townsfolk listened as the wingless Quine began to speak, but his words were unnecessary. It had become increasingly clear that the wet nurses had nothing to do, and most in the town were certain they never would again. Other elders took their turns to speak, but most townsfolk had stopped listening, and alone or in small groups they drifted off into the darkness, until, at long last, there was only the bruised whiteness of the empty Common beneath the cold winter moon.

ROBERT DAVIES

ROBERT DAVIES writes stories about lobster girls and laser beams. Mimetic fiction is for wimps. Raised on a steady diet of weird paperbacks, Infocom games, and comic books, Rob has always wanted to be a writer (Well, actually, he first wanted to be a dinosaur, but that didn't work out so well). When not writing, Rob likes to travel around the world, searching for the ideal pint and the perfect bookstore. He lives in Somerville, Massachusetts, with his wife Sara and two cats, Lilith and Tiamat. His favorite Horseman is Pestilence.

Visit Rob online at *www.robertedavies.com*.

BOOK 1
Jake Burrows
Hiram Grange & the Village of the Damned

Something wicked walks the streets of the picturesque New Hampshire village of Great Bay—something that has inexplicably risen from the grave to wreak a horrifying vengeance. Only one man can stop it—Hiram Grange—provided he can sober up long enough to answer the call!

BOOK 2
Scott Christian Carr
Hiram Grange & the Twelve Little Hitlers

Hitler has escaped. Twelve of them, to be precise, each cloned from the original, and hiding in the bizarre American underground. Hiram Grange has been tasked with hunting them down. The only problem: he's hit rock bottom. His worst binge ever— a mad dance with absinthe, opium and depression …

BOOK 3
Robert Davies
Hiram Grange & the Digital Eucharist

From its global headquarters in Boston, the mysterious Occlusionist Movement is preparing to control the world with its Digital Eucharist, while in the serpentine bowels of the city an ancient demon is unleashed, eager for revenge against the man who imprisoned it years ago—Hiram Grange!

BOOK 4

Kevin Lucia

Hiram Grange & the Chosen One

Hiram Grange doesn't believe in fate. He makes his own destiny.
That's a good thing, because Queen Mab of Faerie has foreseen the
destruction of the world, and as usual ... it's all Hiram's fault.
He must choose: kill an innocent girl and save the universe ...
or rescue her and watch all else burn.
Just another day on the job for Hiram Grange.

BOOK 5

Richard Wright

Hiram Grange & the Nymphs of Krakow

Hiram Grange was already broken when his world was turned
upside down by the horrifying revelations of a beautiful and
dangerous woman. Faced with the possibility that he's been a pawn
in a diabolical game, he seeks the truth in the snows of Krakow.
But the truth is guarded by ancient, winged things,
and the truth has teeth ...

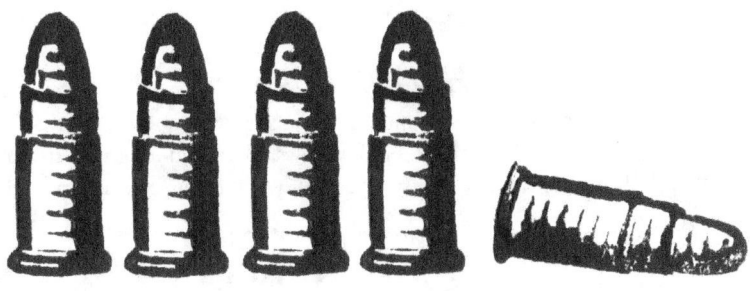

WWW.HIRAMGRANGE.COM